THE FINAL VISIT TO...

DOYLE'S CASEBOOK

Ann Brady

Copyright Written Work: © Ann Brady 2021
Copyright Images: © Ann Brady 2021

Publisher: Pen & Ink Designs 2021

ISBN: 9781915086006

CONTENTS

OTHER WORKS BY THE AUTHOR

Fiction:

Dear Friends: Letters From Abroad – Historical Fiction

Doyle's Casebook – Edition 1 – Crime Fiction (retired)
Doyle's Casebook… Revisited – Crime Fiction
Doyle's Casebook… Another Visit to – Crime Fiction

Little Friends – Picture Books
       Woodland Adventures Series of 6 books
       Garden Adventures   Series of 6 books
       Farmyard Adventures Series of 6 books

Little Friends Colouring Book

Dracula: The Untold Story – Mystery/Horror Fiction
  (co-written with Rex Greenwood, dec'd)

WHO IS TOMMY DOYLE

Tommy Doyle is an ex-Detective Inspector in his mid-forties. He lives alone in an old three-story, brownstone building, in a district of LA. Tommy joined the police force after leaving school, much the same as his father and grandfather had before him.

During his time in the force, he met, fell in love with, and married a sweet girl called Mary. Much to both their regrets, they never had children, and as such Mary found the loneliness and stress of being a policeman's wife unbearable. There were many nights when Tommy didn't come home with Mary not knowing if he was alive or not. Doyle mixing with an assortment of bad guys often frightened her so in time, she came to hate his job.

The final straw for Mary came when Doyle's partner, Pete Mackintosh, came close to being shot dead. Fortunately, Doyle had turned the corner at just the right moment, saving his partner from some mad nutter who thought it would be fun to shoot a cop. The incident created a strong bond of friendship between the two men, which still existed to this day. But for Mary, it was the end; she couldn't take it anymore.

Telling Tommy they had drifted apart she made him choose - her or his job. It was a hard decision for Tommy; but even so, Mary wasn't surprised when he actually chose the job. Fortunately, they parted amicably. Mary eventually married a grocer and lives somewhere upstate. They also have three children, so she is happy, and for Doyle, that is all that matters.

After Mary left she would often ring him, checking up to see how he was doing. As time passed the calls slowly petered out. It had been nearly ten years now since they had seen or spoken to each other. If truth be known Tommy did occasionally miss Mary. It had been nice to come home to a warm house and a cooked meal. 'Oh well,' he had thought, 'it's all water under the bridge.'

Having left the force over three years ago; disillusioned and disappointed, Tommy had become a PI - setting up Doyle's Investigations. He had been a police officer for close to twenty years but had been driven out. Like Tommy and his pal Mac, most of his fellow officers believed he had been set up, but they couldn't confirm that.

It had happened whilst Tommy was working undercover.

Six months into the job he had discovered someone was trying to involve him in a criminal setup. Following twelve months of being investigated Tommy had been hauled before a disciplinary committee. He'd only just managed to avoid being incriminated when a surprise witness had come forward and exonerated him. Still, the whole experience had left a very sour taste in his mouth.

As it turned out, both he and the other officers at the precinct knew a local con man had been involved, although the guy had somehow managed to avoid capture. Perhaps he had been forewarned and had fled the state, leaving Doyle's fellow officers with suspicions that someone within the force was behind the whole affair. Unfortunately, it was something they couldn't prove or follow up on, as connections with those 'upstairs,' meant the guy was protected.

About four months after being cleared Doyle made the decision to retire, or maybe he'd resigned due to being let down by those upstairs? It all depended on your point of view. Being disillusioned, and with the lack of support from senior management, it seemed it wasn't what you knew, but more a question of who you knew. He also found he didn't like the politics of the modern police force.

'I know who you are,' thought Doyle as he walked away from the precinct. 'And one day, you will pay. One day, wherever you are, I will get revenge.' Not that Doyle was one to bear grudges, but he never forgot where a debt was owed; either by him or to him.

As it turned out leaving the police force worked out quite well for Tommy. He'd set up his office on the first floor of the old brownstone building he called home. He had used his savings to renovate the rooms, setting up an apartment on the top floor. His office and a smaller bedroom and bathroom were on the second, with offices on the ground floor. Eighteen months later a relative passed away, leaving him with a sizeable inheritance. It was at this point that the brownstone came into Tommy's possession. Nor did Tommy have to work anymore if he chose not to.

Being a PI could sometimes be dangerous, so Doyle decided to adapt the building, making it more secure. He'd had a small brick extension built at the back of the brownstone. To ensure secrecy he had used the services of a builder from out of town. The extension contained a hidden staircase that ran from the top floor to the underground garage. To complete the job, a secret door leading to the staircase within the extension was installed in a store cupboard in his office. By the time the extension was finished anyone visiting would be unaware of the buildings' secret. The idea of this secret entrance/exit would give him an alternate escape route, should he ever need one? So far, he hadn't used it. But, you never knew what might happen. There was also a staircase to the underground garage from the ground floor.

Doyle's office not only had a bedroom, kitchen and a bathroom, but extra rooms for storage, and a gym. Eventually, he ceased renting out the converted the two ground-floor office units.

Over the last few years, Tommy had enjoyed being a PI. He still had links to the police force through his good friend Mac who occasionally helped him out with some bits of information; all unbeknown to the man in charge at that time, one Lieutenant Johnstone. Mac knew Johnstone disliked Tommy but still, it didn't stop him from helping his mate out when necessary. Mind you Mac wasn't the only one, as his colleagues were not averse to dropping the odd helpful bit of information when

Tommy needed it; obviously when the Lieutenant wasn't looking.

Regardless of missing working on the Police force, and being around the guys he'd known for so many years, Tommy had slowly built up quite a solid reputation within his local community. His favourite place to eat and hang out was O'Malley's Bar & Diner. A middle-aged Irish couple ran the bar; Pat O'Malley and his wife Molly, who cooked the food. She made a 'mean' Stew & Dumplings, Tommy's favourite. The fact Doyle was an ex-copper wasn't held against him, and in fact, probably helped as it made the community feel much safer knowing he lived close by.

Update:

Time has moved on and Tommy has been a PI for quite some time now, but age is catching up with him. And not just him, but his close friend, Mac, Inspector Pete Mackintosh. There comes a time in every man (or woman's) life when they need to assess their future. Is this that time for Tommy Doyle?

Plus, in recent months, Doyle has found his mind wandering towards the delights of female company. And to one lady in particular. The delightful Dr. Veronica Martin, M.E. Could there be romance in the air for Tommy, or is he, as he thinks, too old to start the dating route again? Will this be the time for Tommy Doyle to find some female company? Who can say. It's a question of wait and see. But, for how long?

In the meantime, Tommy still has some mysteries to resolve. Read on to discover what cases he resolves and what the future holds for Tommy Doyle, Private Investigator...

CAT & MOUSE

Doyle was feeling well pleased with himself. He had completed a particularly boring piece of investigative work, which had taken over a week to resolve but the payment had been well worth it. Now he was looking forward to having a few days' rest, and that would start down at O'Malley's Bar & Grill, with his favourite meal of Irish Stew and Dumplings.

Picking up the phone he rang his pal, Mac, Inspector Pete Mackintosh, at the local police precinct.

"Whoa, there, Tommy lad. What can I do for you?" Mac had greeted him warmly in his soft Scottish brogue, which he still had, despite the number of years he had lived in LA.

Tommy laughed. "You're in a good mood, Mac."

"Sure am! We've just put three of Grimondi's boys away for intimidation, so me and the guys are feeling well pleased with ourselves. Are you joining us for a game tomorrow night?"

Tommy laughed again. "It's a date. Tell Curly I intend winning back what I lost to him last time!" Both men laughed at the joke, as they knew the rivalry that existed between Curly and Doyle was all a bit of fun. "Anyway, seeing as how you're in a good mood, and up for a celebration, do you fancy joining me for a bite to eat at O'Malley's this evening? I'm paying." Tommy waited for Mac's response.

"You're on. See you about seven? Ok?" Doyle said fine and hung up the phone.

Tommy sat and thought about Mac. He was pleased his pal had pulled one over on the Grimondi family, especially as Jo-Jo, the new Don, had been getting a bit too big for his shoes lately. Pulling his boys in would certainly up the morale of the guys at the precinct. He was sure they would give him all the details tomorrow night at their regular poker game.

An hour later, Tommy, strolling into O' Malley's, was greeted by Pat, the owner. "Want a table, Tommy?" he asked, his Irish accent seemly thicker than usual.

Tommy nodded his head as he took a seat at the bar. "Yea, but Mac will be joining me shortly, so I'll order when he arrives." He didn't have long to wait.

As soon as Mac turned up, they ordered their meal, got a drink and the pair sat down to chat. "So Mac, tell me what happened."

"Well… we got some info that three of Jo-Jo's boys were threatening a new shopkeeper downtown. Unfortunately, for them, they picked on the wrong guy – ex-Navy Seal. His brother, also a Seal, was visiting at the time. The pair took the three Grimondi guys down fast; certainly surprised them. They called us in and we arrested 'em. The guy who owned the shop had it all on CCTV, so Jo-Jo's lawyer couldn't argue with the arrest."

Laughing, Tommy said, "Well done them. Let's hope that will teach Jo-Jo to stay away!"

After Doyle and Mac had had their meal, they drank up and saying bye to the O'Malley's they headed back to the brownstone, Doyle's home, and office. As they approached the building a woman hesitantly stepped forward. "Mr. Doyle?" she asked in a small voice.

Stopping to look at her, Tommy saw a petite woman in her early thirties. She had long blonde hair and blue eyes. Striking as she was, what struck him most, was the gaunt look on her face. "Yea, I'm Doyle. What can I do for you?"

Swallowing hard. The young woman looked as if she was ready to run. It took her a minute or two to gather herself together, before finally managing to speak. In a whisper, she said, "Janice, the accountant, says you might be able to help me," and she looked around as if she was searching for someone who perhaps shouldn't be there.

Doyle waited a moment, looking around himself, then said, "Why don't you come inside and tell me what the problem is? This is my friend, Mac, he's a police officer, he's off duty, but you're perfectly safe with us," and he smiled reassuringly as he led her inside the building.

Having made coffee, which helped settle the young woman's nerves, the three of them sat down in Doyle's office. They waited as she introduced herself. Then she began to explain her problem.

"My name is Maria Garcia. I'm divorced, and I live alone in Fullerton. Three days ago I woke up with a terrible headache. I've had an odd one or two before. Too much enjoyment from a night out with the girls." and she laughed lightly. "Nothing to worry about, I thought. I took a couple of Migraleve and went to work. Normal day, you might think. Only… it wasn't. When I arrived, everyone started asking me how I was feeling? Was I better? Where had I been? Why hadn't I rung in to say I was sick?"

She paused, but Tommy and Mac didn't speak. Continuing, she said, "I was surprised, as I couldn't understand what they were on about. Then my boss called me into his office, and he asked me the same questions. I told him I didn't understand. I'd gone home on Friday, had a good weekend, and was back at work Monday morning. He looked at me as if I had gone mad. Then he asked me what date did I think it was? Well, I know I had a headache but even I knew it was Monday 5th June."

She stopped and looked at Doyle and Mac in turn. "You see, it had been my friend's birthday on the Saturday – the third. He didn't say anything at first. Then he dropped a bombshell. He told me the date was… Monday… the third of… July." She paused again to allow the information to sink in. "I thought he was joking. That is until he showed me the date on his computer. Mr. Doyle, I don't know what happened, but it seems I've not been at work for a month. And the thing is, I don't know where that month has gone." At this point Maria burst into tears, and sobbing, she concluded with, "The very idea that I have lost 4 weeks… frightens me. I need help, please, to find out where I've been," and she finished on a whisper, tears rolling down her face.

Mac, quick to react, pulled a clean hanky from his pocket, offering it to her, asking, "Have you seen a doctor, Maria?

Wiping her face, she looked up at him. "Oh! Yes. That's where I've been for the last couple of days, having blood tests, examinations for injuries, etc. But the doctors say they can find nothing wrong. I think I'm going to go mad if I don't find out what happened to me," and once again her voice trailed off to a whisper. "Can you help me... please?"

Mac looked at Tommy, letting him take the lead, after all, this was his office and his potential client unless, of course, she chose to ask the police for help.

Finally, Tommy spoke, "Well, Maria, it seems you have quite a puzzle. You're sure the doctors said no injuries?" Maria didn't reply, just nodded her head.

"Mmm... most unusual," said Tommy. "I just need a moment to consider what you've told me. Drink your coffee, and if you want to wash your face there's a bathroom through that door," and he pointed across the room.

Maria nodded her head, and standing up she looked to where he was pointing. As she crossed the room, she said, "All the blood tests came back negative."

"Mmm... strange one. Erm... Where are you staying at the moment?" Tommy asked.

"With Janice. She suggested I didn't go home, or stay on my own. Unless you thought it was okay, she said."

"No... no... Janice is right. You are better staying away from your home for now. As it's too late for us, for me, to do anything this evening, I'll walk you back to Janice's. We'll meet up again in the morning. Can you come back here at about ten? Okay?" and he smiled to help her relax. She nodded her agreement.

* * * * *

Returning from escorting Maria to Janice's apartment, which was above the Mini Market, Tommy asked Mac what he thought about the tale they had just been told.

"Seems a weird one, Tommy. IF... it's genuine then something is wrong. Do you think you can help her?"

Shrugging his shoulders, Tommy, replied, "I can but try. But, as you say, it's a weird one. Ah, well, time to hit the sack. You staying, Mac?"

"I'd better," he laughed. "Wouldn't do for the Chief Inspector of Police to get stopped for a DUI would it?"

Doyle laughed. "Well, in that case, we might as well go upstairs to the apartment, watch some Columbo, and finish the last of that Jefferson's Ocean Bourbon, Pat gave me for Christmas. What d'ya say?"

"Lead on, Tommy lad, lead on," and laughing, Doyle switched off the office lights and they went upstairs.

* * * *

The following morning, despite having finished the bottle of Bourbon, Doyle and Mac were both up bright and early. Mac had left for the precinct, with Doyle settled in his office by the time Maria arrived. She was accompanied by Janice Bartholomew, the local accountant. Doyle felt Janice had a soft spot for him but so far had not shown her interest. If he were honest he was glad, as his interests lay elsewhere, with one very attractive Medical Examiner!

"Good morning, Tommy!" Janice spoke warmly but in a very business-like voice. "I understand you are going to try and help my friend, Maria?"

Tommy smiled. "If I can, Janice; if I can. Take a seat Maria and let's go over things again. You staying, Janice?"

Shaking her head, Janice replied, "No, I'm off to see a client. You're in good hands, Maria. Trust Tommy, he's a good guy," and after pecking Doyle on the cheek she quickly left the office, waving as she closed the door.

"Okay, Maria, let's get started?"

For the next hour, Tommy listened while Maria retold her unusual story. Once she had finished, she sat back and relaxed. It was as if a great weight had already been lifted from her shoulders. Tommy had sat taking notes, now he studied them in silence, asking the odd question now and again to clarify something. After about forty minutes he sat back and looked at Maria.

Finally, he spoke. "Okay, Maria. The first thing we are going to do is go to your place and have a look around. While we're there, I want you to pack some clothes. I'm going to move you into the upstairs apartment, here in this building."

Shock spread across Maria's face. "Why, Mr. Doyle? Do you think I'm in danger?"

Tommy didn't want to frighten her, so he shrugged his shoulders, pulled a slight face, and spreading his hands, said, "Probably not, but... better safe than sorry. Besides, it will make me feel more comfortable knowing I don't have to worry about you being on your own. Okay?"

Accepting his reasoning, Maria agreed to his suggestion, thinking, 'Maybe, Janice was right, She could trust this man. She hoped so.'

As they left the brownstone and headed across town towards her apartment, Doyle said, "By the way, you call me either Doyle or Tommy. I haven't answered to Mr. Doyle for some time now," and he smiled to help her relax.

While Maria packed a suitcase and arranged for the neighbour to look after her pet cat, Doyle inspected the house. Something didn't smell quite right to him. His police nose was twitching like mad, so he felt a call into Mac might be warranted. However, he chose not to tell Maria about his concerns. Once Maria was ready, they returned to the brownstone. Leaving her upstairs to settle in, Doyle went down to the office to ring Mac.

Getting through to his pal, he quickly told him what he needed. "You really think that's necessary, Tommy?"

"I do, Mac. The old nose was twitching like it was ready to drop off. I'll leave the key at Marco's. I'm going to take Maria out for lunch at O' Malley's. We'll do some shopping first for the apartment and I'll leave the key. I'll pick it up later. Catch up with you at the poker. Thanks for helping out"

"Okay, Tommy. Will do," and the call finished.

Tommy's next call was to Janice asking if she would come and sit with Maria in the apartment tonight as he had to go out. Normally, when on a job, Tommy would miss the poker night, but he wanted to discover if Mac had found anything out at Maria's apartment, without letting her know just yet what was happening. Janice agreed, saying she'd be there by seven.

Calls finished, Doyle checked Maria was settled and ready for lunch. He wanted her to feel relaxed. That way, if she remembered anything she had forgotten or omitted to tell, it might prompt her to open up to him. As it happened her mind remained blank, despite her best efforts to recall anything.

"Don't worry, for now, everything will return soon enough, let's get some shopping ordered and go for lunch." Doyle tried to sound reassuring.

* * * * *

Later in the afternoon, as Doyle was about to go down to his office, Maria stopped him, saying, "You know, Tommy, I think I can remember some things."

Doyle smiled, "Told you things would come back, slowly. Come on, sit down on the couch and tell me what you can remember."

Having sat, Maria started, "I remember finishing work on Friday at the usual time. I went home, called for some shopping, and had an early night. I knew I would be late home on Saturday. I got up the next morning, went and had my hair done, had lunch with my twin sister, and then back to my apartment to get ready for my friend's birthday night out." Maria stopped to think. To her, everything was just as she had said it was. It was all normal.

After a short time, she continued. "I wore a black dress, high heels, and carried my blue coat with me. The taxi arrived just before seven-fifteen, dropping me off just after seven forty, at the Blue Lagoon Bar and Grill. I was one of the last to arrive. The evening was great. We had dinner, drank, and danced the night away." She stopped talking. As if thinking about the evening. A frown crossed her forehead. She looked as if she was trying to remember something important.

"What is it, Maria?" asked Doyle gently. "What is it you can't remember?"

Looking at him, Maria appeared puzzled. She was trying to recall something, but whatever it was it was certainly avoiding her. "Tommy, I can't seem to remember what happened next. I know we were dancing. My friend, Linda, was flirting with a guy from the bar. I was talking to Tom from accounts. When I turned around, Linda was gone. I presumed she had gone to the loo. The guy was still stood at the bar, but now he was watching me. After about five minutes, he came over and asked me to dance. Linda was nowhere to be seen so… I said yes…"

"Do you know who this guy was? Did you get his name?"

"I think… he was called… Gerry, but I'm not sure. I know we danced real close. A bit later I saw Linda leave with Tom, so when Gerry asked if he could take me home, I… err… I said yes." Maria stopped talking. Suddenly she started to panic. "Oh, my God. Do you think he did something to me? Maybe drugged me?" And the tears began to flow as she realised what an idiot she might have been.

Tommy was a bit worried. While not wanting to worry Maria, he knew he had to ask some very awkward questions. Swallowing, he took a deep breath, and asked, "Maria, did you sleep with the guy?"

Maria didn't answer. "I don't know. But, I think I must have. Normally, I'm usually quite careful. I wasn't going to invite him inside the building, but I came over all dizzy so he offered to help me to the lift…" and her voice trailed away as she tried to remember that night.

"Err… Can I ask, did the Doctor do a test for sexual intercourse, Maria."

"What! I… I… err… no, I don't think so, I don't know. Oh, my God. Do you think I might have been raped, Mr. Doyle?" she whispered.

Tommy didn't answer. He couldn't say and didn't want to suggest it, especially if it wasn't true as he could see how upset she was. Finally, he said, "Would you object to having an internal examination, Maria. I could arrange for it to be a woman doctor."

"I… I… but won't it be too late? I've had at least six showers since I went to the doctors for the tests."

"Let's see what my doctor comes up with, shall we?" said Tommy. "You may or may not have. This Gerry guy could have been the perfect gentleman. Who knows? But, I want to be sure. For now, I want you to get some rest. However, if you do think of anything else, let me know, please. Okay? Right, Janice will be here shortly to keep you company. I have to go out for a while, and I don't want you to stay on your own. I'm going to go down to the office now to make a couple of calls. Will you be alright?" Maria nodded, still worried about what might have happened but she did feel safe with Tommy.

Leaving Maria to rethink what had happened during and after her friends' party, Tommy went down to his office to speak with Veronica Martin, the precinct's medical examiner. After explaining what he wanted, she agreed to speak to Mac and then pop over to Doyle's brownstone to examine Maria. Tommy then spoke to Mac, filling him in further on his thoughts. Putting the phone down he spent the remainder of the afternoon going through his old notes. There was something niggling and irritating in the back of his mind and he wanted to try and discover what exactly it was. By the time Veronica arrived, he was no further in settling his thoughts.

"Afternoon, Tommy," came a sultry voice.

Tommy looked up to see Dr. Veronica Martin M.E. watching him from the office doorway. She smiled at him.

"Good- afternoon, Veronica," he said smiling back.

The doctor was wearing a tight-fitting red dress which clearly showed every curve of her tall slender figure. Her normally tied-up hair was now flowing down her back, making her look every bit the sultry, sexy lady she was. Laughing slightly, Tommy said, "I didn't know you dressed like that under your white coat, Veronica, otherwise I would have visited the morgue more often. Very nice. Very nice, indeed."

The doctor laughed. "Why, Tommy Doyle, I do believe you are flirting with me. Well, I never. You do surprise me. If I'd known all it took was a slinky red dress to get you to be so complimentary I would have worn one ages ago," and she laughed lightly at him as she crossed the room. Reaching his desk, she bent over to gently kiss him on the cheek. "Mmm… you smell nice."

Tommy laughed. "I never realised what a temptress you were, Doc. You should be careful or I could forget I'm supposed to be a gentleman," and he laughed again.

Veronica looked into his eyes, then straightening she put a serious look on her face. "Okay, Tommy, where's the young woman you want me to examine?"

Doyle stood up. "Follow me, she's upstairs," and he led the way to the upper apartment where Maria and Janice were sat watching TV.

Entering the room, Doyle announced, "Maria. This is Dr. Veronica Martin. She's the precinct's M.E. and she's the lady who's going to examine you and take some samples if that's okay. If you want Janice to stay, say so, otherwise, she can join me downstairs for a coffee in the office?"

"I'll stay if that's okay, Tommy. I think Maria would like that." Maria did not reply just nodded her head in agreement.

As Tommy left the apartment, he heard Veronica say, "Forgive the way I am dressed, but I am on my way out. However, I've brought my overall with me. Now, Maria is it, I can call you Maria, yes? Would you mind undressing? I will be as careful and as delicate as possible."

Reaching his office, Tommy settled down to wait until the Doc had finished. He'd just made a second cup of coffee when Mac arrived. "I thought I would call to see how things are going?"

"Just waiting for Veronica to do her stuff, Mac. Coffee?"

"Yea… thanks." The pair sat down, drinking their coffee in silence.

Three-quarters of an hour later, Veronica walked into the office. "All done, Tommy. I've got everything I need. I'll run the tests on the samples and get my report to you." She stopped speaking, walked further into the room, then gently and quietly closed the door. "I'm sorry to say you were right, Tommy. Heaven knows if she realises she had sex or not. I suppose it's a Godsend that she can't remember. Sorry, it's not good news. I'll let you both have a copy of my full report asap."

Tommy blew his cheeks out in frustration. Hell, he had so wanted to be wrong. "Not your fault, thanks, Veronica. I'm not going to mention anything until I get your report. I need to work out how we go about sorting this out. And I think Mac, you need to be involved. It's going to be tough on Maria."

Mac sat nodding his head. He hated these sort of cases but he sure as hell would get this Gerry guy if he had to. Taking advantage of a drunk woman was bad enough. But, drugging her was another thing entirely.

"Okay, Tommy," said Veronica, smiling. "I'll pop the samples into the lab on my way out. And I'll also speak to the hospital where Maria had her tests to get their samples and results. I'll probably look for drugs they hadn't thought of. Night Mac, night Tommy," and she kissed both of them in turn on the cheek before leaving the brownstone.

Neither man spoke, nor moved until a small knock sounded at the office door. "Come in," yelled Tommy.

As the door opened, Maria asked, "Has the doctor gone, Tommy?"

"Yes, Maria, she has. Is there a problem? Come in, it's only Mac who's with me?"

"I… I think I remembered something. About that night."

Mac and Doyle looked at each other, although neither spoke. Finally, Tommy said, "Sit down. Tell me, what it is you remember?"

After she had sat down, Maria said, "After we arrived at my building, I remember opening the door, then turning to say goodnight, that was when I went dizzy. And when Gerry laughed and offered to help me to the lift. It was as we walked down the corridor that I started to feel really funny. Everything became hazy. I thought I was going to pass out. Later, I thought I must have, but the next thing I remember I was lying on the bed. The room was spinning. The strange thing is it didn't look like my room. The… the wallpaper seemed a different colour. Anyway, I must have passed out again. When I woke in the morning, I was naked in bed and my clothes were strewn across a chair. I must have got undressed, but I honestly don't recall doing it. I'm sorry, that's all I can remember."

Tommy looked at Maria for a few seconds before speaking. "That's all right, Maria. Look I don't want you to worry about it. Don't force it. Your memory will return in due course. Until then just relax. Okay?"

She stood up. "I will Tommy. Thank you. You make me feel safe," and she turned to leave the room.

"Remember, Maria, I will look after you and make sure no harm comes to you," said Tommy.

Turning, she smiled. "That's what the Doctor said. She said you were a good man who would see me right. Thank you."

After the two ladies were settled, Mac and Doyle headed to Curley's place for their usual poker night. The conversation would be serious tonight. They generally tried not to talk shop on these nights, but sometimes it was necessary, especially when Doyle was involved in an investigation of theirs, as any action he took was sometimes off the record, unofficial.

Returning to the brownstone earlier than usual from a poker night, Doyle checked in on the two ladies upstairs. Both were sound asleep, so he left them, returning to the small apartment attached to his office on the first floor. It took him some time to get to sleep, as his mind was whirling. What exactly had happened to Maria? That was the question; one he fell asleep with while still trying to resolve it.

* * * * *

The following morning Doyle was up early, having had a restless night.

"You look a little rough, Tommy," announced Janice as she popped her head around the office door. "Late night?"

"Doyle grimaced. "You could say that. Err... Janice, can I ask you something?" He waved her inside, indicating she should close the door. "Has

27

Maria said anything to you? Has she recalled anything?"

Janice shook her head, looking at him questioningly. "Do you know what happened to her?"

Not wanting to say too much, Tommy shook his head. "Not sure. Got a couple of ideas but don't want to share and get her worried if no need due to her memory loss. Okay?"

"Okay," replied Janice. "Understood. I'm sure you know what you're doing, Tommy. Thanks."

The rest of the day for Doyle was spent researching his old case files. He had been lucky that he had been able to retain copies of his notes and the files from when he was on the job. This had proven useful on more than one occasion. Unfortunately, nothing was rearing its ugly head at that moment. Doyle was becoming frustrated. He had advised Maria to take some sick leave, telling her boss she must have been ill after all. "Tell them you picked a bug up and don't want to spread it around work. That should give you leeway to take as long as necessary. If you need to keep yourself occupied I am sure we can find you something to do?"

Maria had laughed, probably the first time since she had come to Doyle's place. "It's okay, Tommy, Janice is going to bring me some accounts to work on. I do the same type of work as her and have helped her out in the past, so I'm covered. I promise I won't get in your way. Oh! And I can cook too, so I'm happy making us both something to eat if that's okay?"

Tommy smiled, "Sure. Although if you're good you might find Mac popping in now and then. He likes nothing better than a home-cooked meal. That's why he likes O' Malley's. Best Stew and Dumplings ever."

"Well, then I'd better look at calling on my Spanish/Mexican heritage and come up with some tasty tapas dishes as an alternative, hadn't I?" Doyle laughed, it would appear that Molly O' Malley might have a rival for Mac's heart – well for his stomach at least, as he loved Spanish cuisine. Which, Doyle thought, was strange for a Scot? Only time would tell.

* * * * *

The results of all the tests done by Veronica and the hospital arrived on Doyle's desk three days later. In between times, Doyle had been out chatting with his informants to see what, if anything, he could find out about the sex trade. Turned out to be quite a lot. Whether it would be relevant or not only time would tell.

Reading through the reports Doyle was surprised by the results. About to pick up the phone to ring Veronica, the doorbell rang stopping him in his tracks. Looking at the security screen he saw the Doctor herself waiting to gain entry. Letting her in, Doyle went out onto the landing, watching her slowly mount the stairs. She was one hell of a woman. Sensing him watching her she looked up and smiled. Doyle's heart did a backward flip. He hadn't felt anything like that since… since… he'd first set eyes on his ex-wife Mary. And that had been years ago. He'd actually thought his heart was dead.

"And what exactly are you thinking, Tommy Doyle," said the soft sultry voice of the doctor.

Doyle didn't answer immediately, but when he did he surprised both of them. "I was just considering what I would like to do with you? You do realise Doc that you should have a very large warning label hung around your neck?"

Looking at him in surprise, she smiled, asking, "And what would it say, Tommy?"

Smiling back, he said, "Dangerous. Cougar at large. She eats men for breakfast, lunch, and dinner. And… probably for supper as well? Come on in the office, I was just going to ring you."

As he led the way, Veronica followed, smiling warmly and smugly behind his back. 'At last,' she thought. 'I have his attention. Mmm… Tommy Doyle, you've finally woken up to me.' It made her feel good.

Clearing her face and being outwardly business-like, she said, "Okay, Tommy, what appears to be the problem?"

As he sat, Tommy smiled. He too had his own thoughts. 'She was playing games with him. He wanted to bite. But not yet. Mac was right, it did look as if she had the hots for him. Perhaps he should stretch it out a bit. This was going to be interesting.' Instead, he said, "Can you explain what this report means, please? You said she may have been raped.

So, how did you come to that conclusion if she's had had six showers after the event?"

Veronica became very serious. "She was raped but not in the conventional sense. The strange thing is she doesn't remember nor does she have any bad physical after-effects. The reason being is, I think because she was given a muscle relaxant drug. As such she wouldn't feel anything; have no pain as she would be so relaxed there would be no tension against which any force could cause damage. But, having said that there is some slight damage, so yes, she was raped. The question is why? But more importantly, is why was she kept for a month? Now that my darling, Tommy, is your department. Mine was to discover the medical truth. Does that help?"

Doyle sighed. 'Hell,' he thought, although out loud he said, "Yes, and no. Okay, Doc, thanks. I think it might be back to the drawing board. You want a drink?"

Having stood to leave, Veronica leant forward, gently kissed Doyle on the cheek, and said, "Sorry, sweetheart, I have a hot date," then smiling cheekily she floated out of the office and left the brownstone. As she walked down the street to her car she was still smiling. If only Doyle could have seen, he would have been pleased with the effect.

"Damn," said Doyle out loud. She had got one over on him. He was playing it cool and she had swept his feet from under him. Despite that, Doyle now knew the doc was keen on him. As he went upstairs to join Maria for dinner, he chuckled to himself. Should he tell Mac about his encounter with Veronica? No, for now, he would keep it to himself and see how it progressed. However, it appeared as if the game was on, and it was going to be one of cat and mouse. The question though is, who is the cat, and who is the mouse?

* * * * *

The next morning Doyle left the brownstone early. He was off in search of a local informant who had some information for him. They met down a dirty alley close to a metro siding.

"Morning, Pinkie, how's you going? Got some info for me?"

Pinkie was a vagrant who had lived on the streets since leaving the army some twenty-five years ago. Having served in quite a few tours of duty overseas he had never managed to settle back into the normality of living a civilian lifestyle. It had cost him his wife and family. But, Pinkie (short for Charles James Pinkerton, the third, ex-Sergeant Major of the US Marines) was a highly decorated war hero, and he loved the nomadic lifestyle he led. He managed to survive by travelling around picking up odd jobs here and there. Some years ago, Doyle had caught him trying to pawn his war medals so had bought them from him. Doyle had told Pinkie they would always remain his but if he ever wanted to wear them again he just had to come and see him. Pinkie had been grateful, asking Doyle to keep them for his kids, as they were the only things he had that he could leave them that were precious to him. Doyle had agreed and had used him ever since as one of his set of eyes on the ground. Pinkie had served him well.

"Hello, Mr. Doyle. I'm doing well, Sir. And you?"

"Just fine, Pinkie. So what you got for me?"

"I heard you wanted to know about a woman being picked up?" Doyle nodded. "Well," continued Pinkie, "I heard it said that they picked the wrong woman. Should have been someone else. Someone who looks like her. The big Chinese Boss, he's not happy. Thinks the cops will come down on 'em. They're wondering if she remembers anything?"

"Hell, Pinkie, how did you come by all this?" asked a surprised Doyle.

"You know the old warehouse upon east fifty-ninth? Well, I was sleeping in there end of last week, when a couple of cars turned up. I didn't make myself known. Thought it better I stay out of sight. Anyways, out pops the Chinese Boss from one car and some other foreign guy from the other. Looked real mean. They start going at it, verbally. So loud I couldn't help but overhear. Anyways that's what I heard said, Mr. Doyle. Is it any good?"

Taking some money from his pocket, Doyle handed it to the man, saying, "Spot on, Pinkie. Well done, but you be careful. Don't let anyone know you overheard what you did. I don't want to have to come to visit you in the morgue. Okay? Understood?"

Pinkie smiled a toothless grin, "Understood, Mr. Doyle. You's a gentleman. My lips are sealed," and turning he quietly slipped away up the dark alley, hiding his money as went and thinking, he might just sleep somewhere nice tonight. Perhaps in the YMCA for a change. He had soon disappeared into the ether of the smoke coming from local factory.

Doyle sighed. He could only hope that Pinkie would be careful. He had grown a soft spot for the man and would hate to see him hurt. Turning away, Doyle set off in the opposite direction, he was going to head back to the brownstone. He had a worm of an idea wriggling away at the back of his mind and wanted to do some more research before talking to Mac.

As he drove along, Doyle spotted the car tailing him. A black sedan disguised as a private taxi. No mistaking it. They must think he was blind. Coming up to the next corner Doyle noticed the lights were going to turn red. He put his foot on the gas and judging it just right he turned the corner fast. The black taxi stalled at the lights. Not able to get through because of on-flowing traffic. Having turned the corner Doyle took the third street left and then turned left again, before returning into the same road he had been driving on before he'd spotted the tail car. He was now positioned behind the car but shielded by three cars in front. Doyle was now the one tailing.

Once the lights turned green, the black taxi turned left and raced up the street as fast as traffic would allow. They had lost him. Doyle hung back. He wanted to see what would happen next. After checking the various streets along the main road, the black car gave up and headed away. Doyle followed at a discreet distance. Five miles further along the car pulled up, parked, and three men got out, entering a Chinese Restaurant - L'Orchid of Heaven. Doyle parked a little further up the street and finding a phone he called Mac, telling him what had happened.

"Don't move? I'm on my way. And Tommy, do not go inside, do you hear me?"

Smiling at the command in his pals' voice, Doyle answered, "Yea, Mac, I hear you. Don't go inside. Not even for lunch?" and he laughed as he hung up.

Less than fifteen minutes later, Mac and a group of plainclothes officers pulled up outside the L'Orchid of Heaven Restaurant. Doyle quickly joined them. "You packing?" asked Mac.

Doyle shook his head. "Hell, Tommy. Here. If you use it, make sure you lose it," and Mac slipped him a Glock 19, which Doyle quickly hid inside his jacket. "Okay, guys, let's get some lunch."

Despite the opposition to their entry, and comments that the place was full when it was obviously very empty, Mac and the boys walked into the restaurant. As he did a couple of the toughs decided they were going to throw their weight around. But, as they made a grab for Mac, Doyle quickly slipped the gun from his jacket, saying, "I wouldn't if I were you. At this distance I won't miss and he pointed the barrel at the pair of them. Hands down behind your back. I think you'll find yourself under arrest for attempting to assault the Chief of Police."

"Jentlemen… pease… we no need any ploblems here." It was the owner of the restaurant who just happened to be the Big Boss, Pinkie had referred to. After saying something in Chinese to his two guys, they quickly disappeared into the back room. "Pease… come sit. Have a dwink?"

Mac sat, while Doyle remained standing, covering his back. They both refused the drinks offered. Finally, the Chinese man said, in perfect English, "So, officers what can I do for you?"

Mac looked up at Doyle, saying, "It's strange how quickly the accent can change isn't it, Tommy? Mmm… now I wonder why that would be? I want to know why your guys were following my friend here?" and he pointed towards Doyle.

The man tried to smile but it came out as a funny smirk. No-one laughed. "I'm sure you are wrong. My guys, following your friend? I think not."

Doyle was getting frustrated. "Well, tell me then, whose is the black taxi parked out front? The one that the two guys you have just sent out of the room, along with a third guy who entered this restaurant not fifteen minutes ago, were driving while following my friend?"

The man's smirk disappeared. "The men deliver food to customers. Is there something wrong with that?"

Mac waited a few seconds, then standing he said, "As long as that is all they do. Remember, Mr. Cheng." The Chinese man's head shot up in surprise at the mention of his name, although he didn't say anything. Mac continued, "Oh! Yes. I know who you are Mr. Cheng. And I know all about you. Let me tell you this. Your card is marked. If you put one foot wrong in my city, I am going to take you, and your little delivery guys, down – BIG TIME. Do we understand one another?" He paused for effect. "You keep on running your nice Chinese restaurant. But… if I catch you overstepping the boundaries of the law you will feel me dropping like a bomb from on high. Do we understand one another?" The man didn't speak but he had nodded. "Good. Let's go, Tommy?"

As he reached the door, Mac turned, "And one more thing, if you or your delivery guys come anywhere near my friend again, or in fact, any of our friends, you will have the full LA police force to contend with. And I can assure you – you will not like that one little bit. We can make your Triads look like pussycats once we get going, believe me. Got it? Have a good day," and Mac stormed out of the place slamming the door behind him.

Having walked across to Doyle's car, Tommy said, "My hero!" This caused both of them to burst out laughing. "I never knew you loved me that much, Pete Mackintosh," Doyle finished as he slyly passed the Glock back.

Laughing, Mac walked away, calling out after him, "Go to hell, Tommy Doyle."

"Only with you Mac. Only with you," Doyle replied. Then climbing into his car he headed home, keeping an eye out for anyone following him. He just hoped that Pinkie hadn't got caught up in the afternoons' events.

* * * * *

After a restless night, Doyle was up and in his office earlier than usual. Something had been swirling in the back of his mind for a few days. Last night it had suddenly surfaced. Marcia had been reminding him of someone, and he had a good idea who it was. Hitting his computer he had spent his first four mugs of coffee searching for one particular person. Finally, he had found her.

Madame Ellena Martinez – the richest, most successful prostitute in the state of California.

And… by the looks of her… Maria Garcia's twin sister?

"Hell," said Doyle out loud as he picked up the phone to let Mac know he had found his connection.

Having been told the news, Mac's reaction was, "I'm on my way. I'll bring Veronica with me. Better get that lady friend of yours… the accountant. Looks like Maria is going to need all the support she can get," and he hung up without further comment.

Doyle, left with only the sound of the dialling tone, took his time in replacing the receiver. He wasn't looking forward to the next hour or so. He hoped Mac would think to bring a woman police officer trained in handling rape victims, as well as the doc. Until then he was just going to sit and wait. However, first, he needed to print off details about Ellena Martinez.

38

Thirty minutes later, true to his word Mac arrived with Veronica Martin, M.E. and, as Doyle had hoped, a woman Police officer experienced in handling rape victims. Doyle hadn't managed to contact Janice, but had left a message on her answer machine asking her to ring him when she was free.

Before going upstairs the four of them sat and talked over what Doyle had discovered.

"Do you think she knows about this Ellena?" asked Veronica.

"I don't know. That's what we need to find out. So, Mac, who's going to take the lead on this?"

Mac looked up. "It's your case, Tommy, but if you want me to do it then I will. Whatever happens, I think it's going to have to come to us in the end, isn't it?"

Doyle was nodding his head. While he was hesitating in taking the lead, as Mac so rightly pointed out, it was his case and as such he should be the one to talk to Maria. "No, Mac. I'll do it. As you say… it's my case. She came to me for help. Come on then, let's go. By the way, Doc, thanks for being here," and he stood up ready to leave the office.

Veronica Smiled at him. As he passed her she quickly and gently squeezed his hand, saying, "No problem, Tommy. Always willing to help out on a case, you know that. But if you want me to do the talking, I can. Woman to woman! If it helps."

Doyle smiled at her. "Thanks, but this one is down to me," and he led the way upstairs.

As they all entered the apartment, Maria looked up from what she was doing, surprise showing on her face. The look on Doyle's face must have warned her things were not what they seemed, so she quickly piled up her work and moved to sit in one of the chairs by the fireplace. The others had already taken seats on the remaining chair and settee. Maria noticed the woman police officer and smiled at her as she too sat, but on a chair close to the table.

Taking a deep breath, Doyle started. "Maria, I need to ask you some questions."

Looking a little lost, Maria smiled slightly, replying, "Of course, anything. Just ask away."

Swallowing he started, "Maria, do you have any family?"

Although a little surprised by the question, Maria explained about her family or lack of it. She had an older brother. Jose. He was in the army. Away on a tour of duty. Stationed abroad somewhere but she wasn't sure where. Her sister-in-law would be able to give them the details.

Doyle then asked, "What about your parents, or have you any sisters?"

A look of sadness crossed Maria's face as she recalled her late parents. She explained how they had got caught in a gun shootout between two warring gangs. Her father had died instantly, while her mother had died two weeks later. As for her sister. Elli was her name. Well, Ellena really. Her twin. The family hadn't seen her since they were fifteen years old. She had got herself a boyfriend and run away with him. She had never returned.

After her parents died she had tried to find Ellena but couldn't. By this time her brother was due to join the military. So, selling up the family home they split what there was and Maria moved away. She met her future husband, also in the military, not long after, but the marriage didn't last long as she couldn't cope with the possibility of him being killed. Not after the loss of her parents. She was also still frightened that she would lose her brother. In the end, they too had drifted apart, although she had kept some link with his ex-wife.

After a pause, and having gained her self-composure, she asked, "Why did you want to know about my family, Mr. Doyle?"

It was at this point that Veronica took over, being seated the closest to her. "Maria, we know what happened to you."

"You do?"

"Yes, I am afraid we do. It was not nice. Do you want to know? I can tell you if you wish."

Maria looked around, terror was written across her face. She began asking herself, 'Did she want to know? She knew something bad had happened. She hadn't told Mr. Doyle that her memory had started to return, but she had wanted to not believe the visions she was recalling.' Finally, she looked at Veronica and said, "I've been raped, haven't I? And more than once"

Veronica nodded her head, holding her arms out as Maria fell into them, sobbing her heart out. Taking a note of the look on Veronica's face and Kate, the woman police officer who had moved closer to help, Doyle and Mac silently left the room.

* * * * *

Three hours later, Veronica found Doyle and Mac sitting in the office drinking coffee and a shot of Bourbon. Doyle stood up as soon as she entered, not speaking but pouring her a shot of Bourbon and a mug of hot coffee. "We've put her to bed and I've given her a sedative. She'll sleep through the night, but Kate, the young officer will stay with her just in case. Okay, Tommy?"

Doyle nodded his head, "That's fine, doc. Well done and… thanks."

To which she waved her hand in the air as if shooing his comment away. "You owe me dinner," she replied, laughing lightly to relieve the atmosphere.

"Deal, doc. Just name when and where."

Mac stood, "Well if there's nothing more we can do tonight, I'm going to go home and hit the sack. We'll meet up in the morning. Let me know when Maria can talk, Tommy. I want some action. Oh, and thanks for the details about Madame Ellena. Tomorrow, I'll get the vice squad on to finding her and bringing her in. Time we had a serious discussion with that lady," then heading for the door, he said, "Night, Tommy, Doc," and he was gone.

Doyle was a bit surprised. "I thought he might have offered you a lift, Doc?"

Veronica laughed, "So did I. Ah... well, I'll have to get a taxi, won't I?"

Laughing Doyle said, "No, come on my lady, the least I can do is drive you home. And don't worry I've only had the one so I'm still sober."

"What a pity," she replied teasingly as they both left the office.

* * * * *

The following morning, Doyle, up early, was making breakfast when the young officer came into the kitchen. "Morning, Katy, coffee? How is she?"

"Still upset, but she's strong. I think with some help she'll come round. I'm going to talk to the local support officer and see what help we can get her. It's not going to be easy is it, Tommy?"

Doyle shook his head, knowing she was right. He decided there and then he would do his best to make sure she got all the help he could get for her. "How do fancy scrambled eggs and toast?"

Smiling, Katy said, "Please, I'm starving. Didn't get much chance to eat a lot last night."

"What! You should have said. I'd have ordered a takeaway."

"No worries, Tommy. It'll help keep the waistline down," and she laughed.

"It's nice to see two people laughing." It was Maria.

Jumping up, Katy said, "We weren't laughing at you, Maria. Tommy, Mr. Doyle, had been asking me about eating."

"I know. I'm not upset. Err… if there are a couple of eggs to spare I think I could eat something?"

Doyle smiled. "Coming right up, Maria. Take a seat. I am both chef and waiter this morning," and they all laughed, including Maria. It sounded a relaxed laugh, the first Doyle had heard in days.

* * * * *

With breakfast over, Tommy, Maria, and Katy left the brownstone and headed for the precinct. It was time to start sorting this mess out and begin helping Maria rebuild her life.

Before their arrival, the Vice Squad had managed to locate the mysterious Madame Ellena Martinez, bringing her into the precinct where Mac had carried out an interview, with her lawyer present. At first, she had denied any relationship to Maria, however, when Mac had told her she would be held on a number of charges relating to assault, drugs, and perhaps attempted murder, she soon changed her tune. It appeared that she had at first thought that Maria was bringing false charges of assault against Ellena herself. Upon discovering the reality that her sister had been attacked because of her she had finally broken down and a long discussion and explanation had been given. Mac was surprised when she claimed she needed protection.

Meeting with Tommy, Maria and Veronica afterward, he brought them up-to-date on all he had learnt. To say Maria was shocked was an understatement.

"Does she remember me?" asked Maria, warily.

Mac smiled. "Yes she does. She would like to meet you but is so ashamed of what she did when she left home, for what she has done with her life, and for what has happened to you recently that she believes you will hate her."

"She's my sister. How could I hate her? Can I speak to her?"

"You can Maria, but I need to talk to you first. Well, I need to get what happened down on record. I appreciate it will be difficult for you. So to make it easier we have a specialist officer who handles taking statements from victims like yourself. Do you think you are up to sitting and speaking with her? Also, they have some mug shots they would like you to look at. If you can identify this Gerry guy it would help us. If you can't don't worry."

Maria had started breathing heavily. Her heart was pounding. Veronica reached across and held her hand, trying to give Maria some of her strength. Looking up at the Doc, she smiled. Then she said, "Will you come with me, please?"

"If that is okay with Mac and the other officer, then yes I will."

Mac, who had tensed a little, relaxed, saying, "Hell, of course, it's okay. No matter what anyone says, if the Doc here is willing to help you then it's fine by me. Katy, can you show Maria through into the Rape Suite so she can meet Officer Dobson. Doyle and I will see you later, Maria, okay?"

As the three ladies started to leave, Maria stopped in front of Doyle, "Thank you, Tommy," and then she left the room.

* * * * *

After the women had left the room Doyle sat down and let out a long breath. "Hell, Mac, I'm getting too old for this."

"You and me too, Tommy. Right. Do you want to meet the sister and learn some more?"

Shrugging his shoulders, Doyle said, "Why not." Rising the pair left the room and headed towards the interview suite where Ellena Martinez was waiting.

As they entered the room, the lawyer stood up, saying, "About time. Really Inspector, my client has been here for over four hours. She has been very co-operative and would like to see her sister, now."

Mac didn't hesitate with small talk. "Sit down, please Mr. Good. I need to talk to your client some more. As for her sister she is currently speaking with the Rape Officer who is going through her horrific ordeal with her. How long this will take we do not know. So, for now, I expect some co-operation. Okay. Miss. Martinez or should I say, Lopez. That is your real name, isn't it? Now this gentleman here is Mr. Tommy Doyle, he not only represents Mrs. Garcia, but he is also a specialist police officer. If he asks you questions you will answer him, please. Now let's get going."

The interview with Ellena Lopez, aka Madame Ellena Martinez, lasted for two hours. During that time Mac and Doyle discovered, not only her history but a reason as to why Maria had been drugged and attacked.

Once Ellena started talking the floodgates just opened. "I came here about five years ago and with the help of my then-boyfriend, Jack Marston, I set up an upmarket brothel. Everything was great, we started small, with a few select customers, some with quite high profiles, so the money was good. Over time we built up the business, moving into the new premises uptown where your men found me this morning. Times were good. We had a great reputation. The girls were clean and we offered a nice assortment to suit all tastes. Then about eighteen months ago we got a visit from a couple of heavies. Said they were from the Big Boss – a Chinese guy – a Mr. err... Cheng. At first, Jack sent them packing, but over time they started to get heavier in their approach. About two months ago Jack disappeared. I thought he'd chickened out because of Cheng and done a runner on me. I didn't know what to do. I hired a few heavies of my own and managed to keep Cheng at bay. That is, until three weeks ago when I received a box. Inside were Jack's testicles. They'd cut them off. The message was clear. I didn't know what to do. Hey, I couldn't come to you guys? I run a brothel for God's sake. You wouldn't have wanted to hear about my little problem of being threatened would ya? Anyway, about two weeks ago I get wind that Cheng has put a hit of some sort out on me? I didn't know what it was, but I wasn't taking any chances so I went to ground. Closed the brothel and hid. The only reason your guys managed to get me today was that I took a chance on coming back to empty the secret safe I have." Ellena stopped speaking, looking at Mac and Doyle in turn.

Doyle asked, "Did you not know your sister lived in the area?"

"Hell, no. If I had I would have got her out. Besides, after I left home, I only went back once. My Pa told me never to return and to never contact any of them ever again. So I didn't. I didn't even know she had got married."

"She's divorced. That is what's made her vulnerable," said Doyle.

"Look, Mr. Doyle, it's not my fault. I didn't know she was close by, or what her name was. How could I have stopped it."

Mac spoke, "Okay. I want a statement relating to Cheng. By the way, what did you do with Jack's testicles?"

Ellen looked at her lawyer, who nodded. "They're in the bottom of the freezer at the brothel."

"Okay," said Mac, standing. "I'm going to send my Sergeant in. He will take a statement from you. I want details of the dates you were threatened, Jack's death, etc. I also want the keys to the brothel so I can get the remains." Ellena handed over the keys, then Doyle and Mac left the room.

It would take a further hour to resolve the matter. After which both Ellena and Maria would be placed in protective custody pending the arrest of Cheng and, hopefully, Gerry. With nothing left for him to do Doyle returned to the brownstone to write his own records up.

* * * * *

Six weeks later, as Doyle was sat in O' Malley's having a quiet lunch and a drink, a sultry voice said, "Can I join you, Tommy?"

Smiling, Tommy looked up to see Veronica looking down at him. "Any day, Doc. Any day. Want a drink?"

"No thanks. Thought I might find you here. Came to tell you that you are going to have a delivery in about an hour."

Doyle looked questioningly at the Doctor. "Yea! And what might that be?"

"Two special ladies. They're calling to see you before they leave for the safe house upstate. They'll come in the back way if that's okay. It'll be in a black delivery van. Are you gonna be in?"

Smiling, Doyle replied, "How could I not be. A special delivery like that. I'd better get back to the office. Thanks, Doc," and standing he asked her, "You coming back with me?"

"Of course, Tommy, darling. I daren't leave you alone with two delightful, pretty looking young women, dare I?" and she laughed warmly and seductively at him.

'Hell!' thought Doyle as they left the bar. 'Maybe it's me that's the mouse and she's the cat?'

MIRROR IMAGE

The sound of sirens woke Doyle from a delightfully deep sleep. It was a Sunday morning, and he was hoping the noise wasn't heralding a repeat of the time the Mini Market had caught fire. Having passed, silence reigned once more. Doyle attempted to recapture the lost moment of him taking a certain desirable woman into his arms. He was just about to kiss her when the phone by the side of his bed blared out, demanding to be answered.

Sighing, Doyle rolled over, snatched up the receiver, and snarled, "What?"

"Hell, Tommy, you get out of the wrong side of the bed this morning."

Doyle took a slow breath. "I am not out of bed yet and hadn't planned on getting out. What do you want, Smithy?"

The young police officer didn't take offence at Doyle's manner, understanding that the man may well have only been in bed a couple of hours, especially if he'd been out working the previous night. "Mac says, can you meet him at O' Malley's in half an hour? He needs to talk to you."

Doyle sat up in bed, now fully awake. "What about, Smithy?"

"Didn't say. Just said to meet him. Okay? Sorry, Tommy, I got to go. Bye." Doyle was left listening to the dialling tone.

Placing the receiver down, he scowled. It wasn't like Mac to be so secretive, or to not give a clue. Strange also for him to want to chat at O' Malley's.

He looked at the clock – it said five past ten. He sighed again. Then throwing back the covers he reluctantly left his sweet dreams where they were, and headed for the shower.

Exactly on ten thirty, Doyle strolled into O' Malley's Bar & Grill, surprised to discover it full of police officers and forensic personnel, all having breakfast. 'What the hell,' he thought?

"Morning, sleepyhead. Grab a coffee and join me," shouted Mac from a table in the corner.

Doyle did as he was told, joining Mac, who was stirring sugar into the mug of hot steaming coffee he was holding, a few minutes later.

Taking a seat, Doyle asked, "What gives, Mac? Something happened to the O' Malley's?"

"Morning, Tommy," came the sweet Irish voice of Molly O' Malley from behind him. "I saw you arrive, so here you are a fresh cooked egg and bacon sandwich. And one for you too, Mac."

Mac grinned at Molly. "You know how to please a man, Molly O' Malley. I really will have to marry you. Any sauce, please?" Laughing and blushing at the same time, Molly handed over some sachets of sauce to both men, before returning to the kitchen.

Once Mac had taken the first bite of his sandwich, and a drink of the sweet coffee, he looked at Doyle, asking, "Do you remember the Jason Warrington case?"

Doyle thought for a moment. The Warrington murder had been one of his earliest cases after being promoted to Detective Inspector. There had been a problem trying to prove who the murderer was, so the case had stayed open. He and Mac had reviewed the case every year, but with no new evidence, it had remained unsolved. There had been one suspect. However, the man had had a damn good alibi; and even though Doyle was sure he was the killer he couldn't nail him down.

Finally, Doyle spoke. "Yea, I remember the case. The only suspect was Nial... No, Neil... Parton?"

"Yea, that's him. Neil Thomas Parton. Six feet, aged twenty-eight at the time, quite an ordinary guy. He said he only knew Edward Warrington, the son, through a friend of a friend. You thought you had him nailed – until, he came up with the perfect alibi."

"Too damn perfect to my mind, but I couldn't prove any different. So, what's this all about, Mac?"

Mac swallowed before responding. "Neil Parton has turned up again. At least... I think it's Neil Parton."

Doyle scowled and looked at Mac questioningly. "What do you mean, you think it's Parton?"

"Well, Tommy. There's been a murder at Frogmore House. Old man Smithson, Graham, was found murdered three days ago. No one appears to have been near the house for about five days. However, we found out this morning that the old man had installed secret security cameras. Did it without telling anyone, apart from his friend, Martin Jameson. This Jameson has been away on business. Returned late last night to hear the news. Contacted the precinct this morning to ask if we'd checked the security system."

Doyle laughed. "Bet that surprised ya'?"

"Too damn true it did. Apparently, even the son didn't know about the security cameras. I've just come back from meeting Jameson at the house. He showed us where the system was hidden. We gained access and checked the recordings. It was not a pretty sight."

Doyle sat shaking his head in disbelief. "Did you get sight of the murderer?"

"Yea… that's why I wanted to speak to you. I wondered if you'd come down to the precinct and view the tapes with me? Double-check what I think I'm seeing!"

Doyle was surprised. It was rare these days for Mac to call on him to assist in an investigation but, if that's what he wanted, and it resulted in capturing a murderer then he would be there asap. "Sure, Mac. Tell me when and where."

"Okay. How about tomorrow morning?" Doyle nodded his head, agreeing to meet up in the morning. "Tommy, I don't want to get your hopes up. But… if it is Neil Parton. Well, maybe we should relook at that old case of yours. Not promising it will reap the rewards you want but who knows."

Returning to the brownstone, Doyle was eager to review the Jason Warrington cold case. Although officially a police case, he had kept a copy of the file for his own interest. It also made it easier for him to review the records easily, in case he discovered they had missed something. But, despite spending the rest of the day studying the contents of the file nothing sprang out at him.

'I'm looking at this the wrong way,' he thought. 'Time for the *old detective's* help!'

It was strange how watching the TV series, Columbo, often helped Doyle get his mindset sorted. He knew he had missed something but the question was – what? Unfortunately, this time the detective in the scruffy raincoat was no help in settling his mind. As such he spent the rest of the evening sorting out the last of his cases, ready for the typist to update for inclusion in the training manual he was creating.

Retiring later, having worked into the early hours, and having consumed more than one decent shot of bourbon, Doyle did not have a restful night's sleep.

* * * * *

At nine-thirty the following morning, a dull, slightly overhung Doyle, strolled into Mac's office.

"My God, Tommy, you look rough."

Doyle gave a grin of sorts as he sarcastically replied, "You ain't that pretty yourself, Mac."

Mac did not reply. He just pointed to the chair opposite; indicting Doyle should sit down. Having done so he pushed a file of photographs across the desk towards him. "These are the stills from the tapes. They aren't that good as the tapes were of poor quality. Old man Smithson was tight. Bought cheap tapes and reused them over and over again. The guys in tech have done their best."

Doyle looked at the photos. They were a little hazy, showing a man standing over the lifeless body of Mr. Smithson. The other photos showed the same man in different places within the room. He looked as if he was searching for something. Despite the images being hazy, Doyle, like Mac, was sure it was Neil Parton. Certainly an older version, but definitely Parton. 'Hell,' he thought. 'Could it be Parton? It sure as hell looks like him.'

Looking up, he found Mac watching, waiting for his reaction. "Have you picked him up yet?"

"He's on his way in… with his lawyer. Sorry, Tommy… I can't let you sit in on the interrogation… but you can watch through the glass."

Doyle thought for a moment. "No, no, you're right, Mac. Probably better I don't stay. I'm likely to save the county a trial and a conviction. I'll err… head on back to my place and start doing some research. I plan on sorting the Warrington case out, once and for all. Sorry, Mac. I'll see you later,' and on that note, Doyle left the office.

Mac sat back in his chair. He was shocked, and a little disturbed. In all the years he'd known Doyle, he had never reacted in such a way. Parton had a lot to answer for. Mac hoped Tommy would be able to get his mind straight and resolve the matter. He would hate to find his friendship damaged because of an asshole like Parton.

By the time Doyle had returned to the brownstone, his mood had calmed somewhat, and he had started to feel a little guilty at how he had spoken to Mac. He would have to apologise, but for now, he needed to resolve the problem of Neil Parton.

Taking out the Warrington Murder files, Tommy sat at his desk and began reviewing all the forensic evidence, interview statements, reports, interrogation reports, and photos, He laid them out neatly on the table, before pinning each in turn on the viewing board attached to the wall. Bearing in mind the changes in the way the police investigated crime these days to back then, Tommy decided he would go back to the beginning. He would restart the investigation from the start and look at what was missing from the reports, etc.

For the next few days, Tommy concentrated on revisiting the crime scene. Then, deciding to follow up on the interviews, Doyle visited each of the people from the original investigation, starting with Mrs. Dean, the housekeeper who had worked for Jason Warrington. Since her employer's death, she had retired, preferring not to work for the son, whom she apparently thought was a spoilt brat.

Finding her new address was easy and before long he was knocking on her door. Doyle explained who he was and why he was there. Inviting him in she was more than willing to go over her statement, easily recalling the day of the murder.

Having made both Doyle and her a cup of coffee, Mrs. Dean sat down and said, "I can't forget that horrible day. Have you got someone for poor Mr. Warrington's murder?"

"Not yet, although we might have a suspect. That is why I am trying to reinvestigate the crime. What can you recall?"

"Well, my dear, it had been raining, so I was wet when I arrived. I was surprised that Mr. Warrington hadn't sent his new chauffeur to fetch me. I know the young man had only been working for him for a short period of time, but still, Mr. Warrington would often let him pick me up if it was wet. Anyway, by the time I arrived, it had stopped raining. Philip, the chauffeur wasn't in when I got there, so I thought he must have been out on an errand for Mr. Warrington, which explained why he didn't call for me. I opened the door. The alarm was set. Now that was strange. You see, usually, Mr. Warrington had the alarm un-set for when I arrived, so I didn't have to bother. Another coffee, Mr. Doyle?"

Tommy smiled. "No, thanks. I'm fine. What else do you remember, Mrs. Dean?"

"Now, where was I, dear? Oh yes, so, I let myself in, un-set the alarm, and hung my coat up. Err... I went into the kitchen and made some tea and toast for Mr. Warrington, put it on a tray, and... went to take it upstairs, picking the post up off the table on my way. But, when I got to the bedroom, Mr. Warrington wasn't in bed. In fact, his bed hadn't been slept in at all. I couldn't understand it."

"So, what did you do then?"

"Well... I went back downstairs, put the tray in the kitchen, and got on with my cleaning duties. I collected the duster and the hoover from the cupboard, then headed for the study. Oh! You can imagine my shock when I discovered poor Mr. Warrington lying in front of the hearth, dead as a dormouse."

Leaning forward, she placed her hand on Doyle's knee and whispered, "Do you know I almost screamed. But I'm made of sterner stuff than that."

Patting her hand gently, Doyle said, "I'm sure you are, Mrs. Dean, I'm sure you are. So, what happened next?"

Smiling at Doyle for his kindness, and thinking, 'What a nice young man,' she continued. "Well, of course, I phoned the police and they came right over. A nice young detective, tall... like you... Do you know, he looked just like you... only younger? Oh! It was you... wasn't it?"

And smiling at her, Doyle nodded his head. "Yes, Mrs. Dean, it was me. And very helpful you were to me back then. Just as you've been very helpful now. Thank you."

Smiling at Doyle, Mrs. Dean was pleased. "That's good. Now, if I think of anything else, Mr. Doyle, do I ring the precinct?"

Surprised, Doyle shook his head. "Err... no Mrs. Dean. Here's my card. I'm a PI now, but I work with the Police on certain cases, as an advisor. You contact me on this number if you think of anything. Okay?" Then thanking her, Doyle left the lady who felt pleased with her afternoon visitor.

Doyle's next stop was to the local police precinct to catch up with some of his old mates who had been around at the time of the murder. Apart from catching up on the time passed, the guys around at the time of the case chatted about what they could recall. By the time Doyle returned to the brownstone, he was feeling both pleased, but also a frustrated at not being much nearer to resolving the case.

Entering his office, he could see the red light on the answering machine blinking away. Pressing the rewind button, he listened to a couple of messages. The first was from Mac, asking if he was okay, not having heard from him for a few days.

This was followed by one from the precincts ME, Dr. Veronica Martin, also asking Doyle if he was okay. Mac must have shared his worry about him with her.

Doyle smiled to himself. Picking up the receiver he phoned Mac.

"Mackintosh."

"Hey, Mac. I'm sorry about the other day. Things got to me. Fancy a bite to eat and a drink at O' Malley's?"

Mac smiled to himself before responding. "Sure, pal, why not. See you in half an hour at the bar?" Having agreed to meet they both hung up.

Thirty-five minutes later, Mac walked into O' Malley's Bar & Grill, spotting Doyle sat at a corner table drinking a long cool draft beer. "Want another one, Tommy?" he called out.

"It's on the tap waiting for you," Doyle replied.

Collecting two beers, Mac joined Tommy at the table. "Here you go, Tommy. How you doing."

Tommy sighed. He was ready to grovel. "Look, Mac, I really am sorry about the other day. The Warrington case has always got to me. This could be the one that gets away, unless we can nail Parton for the Smithson murder. If we can, well great. Better that than nothing. Any updates?"

Mac knew that what he was about to tell Tommy wouldn't go down well. "Unfortunately, the guys in tech couldn't make the images any clearer, and it looks like Parton has an alibi. A water-tight one."

"What!! Not again. The devil. He can't have. Hell, Mac, we gotta get this perp, somehow. I don't care how we do it. And, I'll bet all my savings that he did it, so we have to prove it."

Mac laughed. "My, you really do not like the guy do you."

"I do not. Will you do me a favour?"

Mac shrugged. "Yea. Just ask."

"Get Veronica to recheck the autopsies for both crimes and compare them to each other. And if possible, re-do the tests etc. Things have moved on. If she can look through the forensic files, she might find something we haven't."

"Sure, Tommy. I'll get her on it first thing tomorrow. And, I'll get her to send a copy of the results directly to you as well as me. Okay?" Tommy nodded his agreement. "In the meantime, Tommy, what are you going to be doing?"

Tommy thought for a moment. "I'll finish going through the interviews etc., and then I'm going back to basics. Going to do some research on our Mr.

Parton. See what I can find out about the guy that we don't know already. Things have moved on. We have internet access now which wasn't around back then. Means he can't hide as easily. And, I have access to records now I didn't have back when Warrington was murdered. Right, let's eat?"

Having settled his mind, Doyle felt much better. Motioning the young waitress over they ordered some food. The rest of the evening was spent in convivial companionship, with both Doyle and Mac feeling their friendship was back on key. Both feeling relieved, as this was the first time in all their years that they had ever come close to any type of disagreement. They each slept well that night.

* * * * *

The following morning, Tommy was up and sat at his desk early. Mac had stayed overnight but had already left for the precinct, having asked Tommy his plans for the day before leaving. Mac would arrange for the M.E. to look at the forensic evidence asap, leaving Doyle to continue his investigations regarding the Warrington Murder.

Around mid-morning Tommy left the brownstone, returning to the area where the Warrington estate was situated. After Mr. Warrington's demise, the estate had been inherited by his son, Edward, who currently lived there with his second wife, and the children from his first marriage. He had divorced his first wife not long after his father's death. 'That's a coincidence,' thought Doyle.

Arriving at Warrington Hall, Doyle was met by a security guard who appeared reluctant to let him in to see Mr. Warrington. Doyle had met his kind before. All talk and no action. They thought of themselves as tough men, just because they had a bit of brawn. Leaning in towards him, Doyle spoke softly, but with a hint of a threat in his voice.

"Now, look here mate. You can either let me in to speak to Mr. Warrington, nice and friendly OR... I come back with a warrant and turn not just the mansion over, but you and your joint as well. I can cause you more problems than you ever think I can. So, what do you want to do? Obstruct someone who is acting on behalf of the police or, do I get a full squad down here within the next thirty minutes and tear this place to pieces? Your decision?"

The guard stared at Doyle, who didn't move or flinch an inch from the man's menacing stare. Then sighing, and with a sour look on his face, the man finally said, "I'll tell Mrs. Warrington you're here. Mr. Warrington is away on business. But he won't like it."

'Tough,' thought Doyle. 'I don't like you, but I'm not crying.'

Five minutes later Doyle was shown into the study of Warrington Hall where he was met by a tall blonde-haired woman, aged in her mid-forties, yet looking ten years younger. She was dressed smartly, as if by someone like Chanel.

"Good day, Mr. Doyle. Thompson tells me you are a Private Investigator. How may I help you?"

"That is correct, Mrs. Warrington. However, I also work as a Police advisor, and as such, today I am representing them. We are looking to re-open the case of the murder of the late Mr. Warrington and I need to ask your husband some questions. Can you tell me when you expect him back from his business?"

Mrs. Warrington had turned pale at the mention of the Police re-opening the case of the Warrington murder. Sitting, she appeared to find it a little difficult to breathe. Finally pulling herself together, she managed to say, "I cannot see how my husband can help you. He was nowhere near here when my late father-in-law was murdered."

"But he wasn't, was he?"

"Wasn't what, Mr. Doyle?"

"Your late father-in-law. You weren't married to Mr. Warrington then, were you?"

"That is a matter of semantics, Mr. Doyle. Just because we weren't married at the time, if he were alive today then he would be my father-in-law, wouldn't he?"

Doyle didn't respond, he just nodded. "Tell me, Mrs. Warrington, when did you meet your husband? Before or after his father's murder."

"Why do you want to know that?" She sounded indignant at the question.

"Because I asked, and it may be relevant. So, Mrs. Warrington, when did you say you met your husband?"

Sniffing and taking some seconds before answering, Mrs. Warrington finally replied, "Edward and I were passing business acquaintances, but we didn't get to know each other until after he divorced his first wife. She was an alcoholic. We fell in love. Edward had the children to look after. I married him to help bring them up. They are both away at university now. Happy?"

"Ecstatic," said Doyle under his breath, with a hint of sarcasm, as he stood and turned towards the window. "Can I see the study where Mr. Warrington was killed? This doesn't appear familiar to me and I wish to renew my memory of the layout, etc?"

Standing, Mrs. Warrington appeared to gather herself together, saying, "No. The old library was changed into a sitting room. His father's study was adapted to be part of a new library. Edward felt it had too many bad memories. This is the new study. It used to be a sitting room."

"Can I see the room, anyway, please?"

Surprise crossed Mrs. Warrington's face. "Why? It is very different to the way it was."

"If you wouldn't mind?" insisted Doyle.

Pursing her lips with indignation, Mrs. Warrington finally said, "Very well, follow me," and she turned to leave the room.

Doyle followed slowly behind, observing everything. Suddenly, he asked, "How would you know what the room looked like before if you didn't meet your husband until after his divorce?"

"I visited the odd Christmas Party here," she replied smugly as she opened the door to the new library. Doyle entered without replying, comparing the room he now saw with the photos he still carried in his memory. It certainly had changed. He searched the room with his eyes finally concluding it had changed so much, there could certainly be no evidence left to find. Deciding it was time he left, he thanked Mrs. Warrington for her time, reminding her that he would still like to speak to her husband. He gave her his business card, asking that he contact him as soon as possible... "It will prevent another visit, this time from the police themselves," was his parting shot.

As he drove away, Julie Warrington stood at the study window watching him leave, a worried look on her face. She knew Edward was travelling back today but, as he was on a plane, she couldn't tell him about the visit until he arrived home. She wasn't sure what he would say about the case being re-opened.

Arriving back at the brownstone, Doyle sat mulling over both what he had, and had not found at the Warrington Estate. Some more research to add to the list. Tomorrow, he would be investigating a few things that weren't originally looked at. If they had missed something during the investigation, then it was down to him to find out. He was hoping they had not but, he began to feel that somewhere he had got it wrong.

Doyle would not have a settled night.

* * * * *

The following morning, Doyle was up and out of the brownstone early. He decided a good breakfast was needed so he strolled down to O' Malley's Bar & Grill for coffee and one of Molly's egg and bacon sandwiches. Sitting mulling the Warrington case over, he was unexpectedly joined by an old colleague, Douwe Korff – Dutch for short. Doyle and Dutch had been at the police academy together, later walking the beat together as partners. After Doyle was promoted, he and Dutch had parted company. Dutch had retired early due to being injured in a police shoot-out with some crazy street gang about twenty years ago. He had walked with a limp ever since.

"Dutch, hell man, how you doing?"

Laughing, the ex-cop strolled over to join Doyle at his table. "Well, Tommy Doyle, as I live and breathe. How are you, Tommy? Looking good. Still married to that lovely girl of yours? What was her name… May… Martha… No, Mary."

Doyle laughed. "Coffee, Dutch?" The man nodded his head. Doyle waved to Pat who filled two mugs with hot steaming coffee and brought them across to the table. "By the way. You're right it was Mary. The word being was. Got divorced some years ago. She couldn't take the job."

Dutch nodded his head and sighed. "Yea, I understand that problem, Tommy. My Gracie left me after I got shot. Said she couldn't live with me being on the job. At the time I thought I would continue

67

but... obviously, they commissioned me out of the force. Gammy leg, you see," and he patted his wounded leg.

Doyle nodded in agreement. It could so easily have been him sat there instead of Dutch.

"So, Dutch, what you doing around these parts?"

Dutch didn't speak for a moment. Then realising that Doyle was an okay kind of guy, he said, "I'm sort working a job. You know, investigating. Trying to trace a pair of twins. Two guys who are so identical, it's hard to tell them apart."

Scowling, Doyle asked, "What they done?"

"Only gone and cheated at least six women out their life savings. Pulled some sort of scam. I'm not sure how they did it, but a couple of the ladies I represent, seem to think that there had to be two of them working in tandem. It appears that the guy would get close to the woman, convince her they were in love, and slowly wheedle his way into her confidence. He would tell her about an investment opportunity that she just couldn't miss, encouraging her to withdraw her money ready to invest, placing it in a secure place hidden in her apartment. It was all top secret, so she couldn't tell anyone. Having done this, he would offer to take her out to eat to celebrate, and stupidly she agreed. He had gained her confidence, and she had foolishly given him her alarm code. When they returned the money was gone. So, no break-in as such. Key used for entry; alarm code used. Police presumed she hadn't set it properly. She couldn't blame her friend as he was in full view of her and forty other diners in one of the best restaurants in town. About a week after the robbery, a woman turns up saying she is the guys' wife and causes a big row. Within two to three weeks the romance has fizzled out and he and wifey have disappeared. Money gone forever.

Doyle scowled again. "So, tell me Dutch, where do the twins come into this?"

Dutch took a long drink of the semi-hot coffee. "When I asked the women to give me a description for the man, they felt had conned them, they all described the same person. Except for two of the women, who appeared a little more observant than the others. It could have been because the others were embarrassed. Anyway, the two women told me that they had been intimate with the guy. Both said that it was the same man except for one time only. It appears that in the act of 'making love' both ladies felt a small mole on the man's lower back. It was only one time, as every other time they were in bed there was no mole. Now, none of the other four ever noticed a mole. I think the two women thought they had imagined the mole. But it got me thinking."

"You can't have a mole one night, and then not the next," said Doyle shaking his head in appreciation of his old pal's attention to detail.

"Precisely," nodded Dutch. "Two men. Both identical in every way to each other. My guess - twins."

Laughing gently, Doyle said, "Well done, Dutch. Pity they didn't give you a desk job, alongside me," and he raised his coffee mug, to cheer the man.

Doyle thought for a moment. He'd suddenly had an idea. He wasn't one hundred percent sure but now he had an angle to investigate further. After a short period of silence, Doyle leant forward and said, "Dutch, do you fancy doing a bit of work with me. I have an idea that your job and mine, might just cross over. Mine is a double murder. Be good to get these twins for the lot. What do you say?"

Surprised, Dutch agreed. He was going to get paid regardless.

Returning to the brownstone, Doyle spent the remainder of the day ringing around gathering details regarding those people involved in the embezzlement, so he could compare them to the murder suspect. Dutch was sent off on errands, collecting various reports and copies of documents from the county's National Center for Statistics. Checking in with Doyle, he was instructed to return to the brownstone.

Suddenly the fax machine whirred. Doyle looking up from the desk, saw several documents printing off. He recognised that they were from the M.E. Dr. Martin. Quickly he gathered all the papers together, making sure they were all in numerical order. No sooner had the pages stopped printing than the phone rang. It was Veronica.

"Hello, Tommy... Veronica Martin here." Despite her being professional in her address she still sounded seductive and sexy.

"Hi, Doc. How's ya doing?"

"Fine, Tommy, fine. Did you get all the pages I sent over? Mac said you wanted them asap."

"I did. Thanks, Doc. I'll study them this evening. If I've any questions, can I ring you?"

"All work and no play, Tommy, makes for a very dull boy. Why don't I come on over and go through the reports with you?"

Laughing gently, Doyle was tempted to say yes, but... "Sorry, Veronica, as much as I would like that, I have company. An old mate is staying for a couple of days. He's helping me out."

"Well, I never thought you would need help for anything, Tommy Doyle," laughed Veronica.

"I have a feeling we are looking for the same guy, or I should say, guys! Take a rain check? Maybe another time?"

"It's a date." And on that note, she hung up.

Placing the phone down on the receiver, Doyle was about to return to his desk when the phone rang again. "You forgotten something, Doc?"

"My, my, my... so Tommy boy, and what's all this with the doc?" It was Mac and he was laughing at the thought of Doyle and the doc getting it together.

"Knock it off, Mac. The doc just hung up. She's just sent the reports over and wanted to make sure I had all the pages. You do have a dirty mind,

Inspector Pete Mackintosh," and despite him trying to remain serious, Tommy couldn't help but laugh.

"Okay, I won't push it. But you know, you and the doc really should get it together. She does have the hots for you. Anyway, what's been happening?" Ignoring Mac's innuendo, Tommy brought his pal up-to-date on what he had not found out, what he was waiting to read, and what he had learnt from Dutch. "Wow, Tommy, you've got a lot further than we have. You ready for a conflab?"

"I haven't put it all together yet. Look, Dutch is staying here and helping me out. Why don't you pop over tonight and help us sort out the info he's bringing back? There's a lot of paperwork to go through, plus I haven't had a chance to read what Veronica has sent over. We could make a night of it. I'll get Molly to send us some grub over from the Bar. Save us going out. What do you say?"

Mac, smiled, he knew Doyle was the real deal and he was about to prove it yet again. "Count me in, Tommy lad. I'll bring the beer and bourbon. See you in three quarters," whereupon he hung up.

About half an hour later, Dutch returned with an envelope full of assorted papers that he'd collected from various places. Not long after, Mac arrived and was introduced to Dutch. The pair hit it off straight away. About an hour later, one of Molly's boys delivered a big pot of Stew & Dumplings and some garlic bread. Along with the beer and bourbon, the three were set up for a good night in.

Having just started sorting and spreading the papers out across the floor, they heard the doorbell ring. Checking the intercom video, Doyle was surprised to see Dr. Martin waiting outside. 'Hell,' he thought, 'What was he going to do?'

Pressing the intercom, he said, "Who's there?"

"Come on, Tommy, you're not blind, you know damn well it's me. It's raining, let me in."

There was little he could do but comply.

He watched as she mounted the stairs to the office. "I've brought dessert. And a clear mind to explain the reports in plain detail. Don't look so glum, Tommy. I am not here to spoil your party, and besides, a woman's view can come in handy!" and she laughed as she pecked him on the cheek as she passed. Tommy smiled to himself, thinking, 'What a woman!'

With introductions over, the coffee, beer, and bourbon poured, the four sat down, each concentrating on a specific area of the investigation. Veronica explained the results of the reports to Dutch and Mac. Doyle listened with one ear as he sorted the papers Dutch had brought back for him earlier in the day. It contained information from the hotels he had rung, copies of birth and baptismal records, wedding and divorce certificates, and finally, school reports and photos from school yearbooks. They all worked in companionable silence, broken only by the odd comment here and there. If something was interesting, it was pinned to the pin-board for further study.

After a couple of hours, Doyle called time, suggesting they go upstairs to have a bite to eat, relax, and clear their minds before starting again. Whilst Veronica set the table, Doyle made sure the Stew was hot and the garlic bread was heated through.

"Great place you have here, Tommy," announced Dutch. "Didn't know a Detec's pay or PI work could run to such things."

Doyle paused before replying, "It can't. I inherited it from my Mother. Belonged to my Grandfather. He was in art and antiques. Used this place as a warehouse, office, and auction place. When he retired it was left empty. Came to me when my Grandmother passed a few years back. Never needed to use it so I rented it out. When I left the job, I thought it would come in handy, and it has. I'll sell it when I give up the PI lark."

Doyle wasn't sure who was more surprised. Him for sharing such private information about himself, Dutch, or Veronica for seeing a side of him they never knew. Even Mac was surprised, as he realised that this was a Doyle he had never known; even after all the years they had spent working together. But then, why would he. They had never talked about personal stuff; not even about what went wrong with his ex-wife Mary.

No one spoke for a while until Veronica, quietly said, "Holds things close to his chest does our Mr. Doyle, Dutch. Very close to his chest. Isn't that right, Mac?"

Breathing a sigh of relief, Doyle laughingly said, "Well, not quite, Doc. After all, I haven't held you that close... yet!" Suddenly the room burst into laughter. Even Veronica laughed, despite her trying to look indignant at him. The mood was lifted, with the rest of the evening flowing easily.

Returning to their work, after the meal, the quartet carried on sorting, discussing, and marking appropriate passages and sentences that would help them sort all the cases out. As one o'clock rolled towards two, Doyle finally called it a night. He gave Veronica his room to sleep in as it had a lock on the door. Dutch already had the other spare room, so Mac and he went downstairs to use the beds in the office-floor apartment. With the help of the beer and bourbon, everyone had a restful night. Well, maybe not Doyle, for he lay awake for a while thinking of one very sexy Doctor lying in his bed, and for the first time, wishing he was there with her.

* * * * *

The following morning Doyle was up early and, in the kitchen, making breakfast when he heard, "Morning, Tommy." It was Veronica. To Doyle, her voice was like maple syrup flowing slowly down his morning pancakes, making him feel as if she was caressing him.

Taking a breath, he pulled himself together, responding with, "Morning, Doc. Coffee and toast?"

Smiling to herself, she knew the effect she had on him, so said, "Just coffee, please, Tommy. A girl has to watch her figure," and she laughed lightly.

"Morning," announced Mac and Dutch in unison as they entered the kitchen. "Great, coffee and toast," said Mac, "Just what I need to set me up for the day." Having helped himself to both, Mac asked, "Ok. So, let's go over what we are going to do? If we don't catch these two pretty damn quick, they may go underground again and we'll lose our chance.

Dutch, Veronica, and Tommy joined Mac at the table and the four of them discussed the plan of action they had come up with the previous evening. "Will this work?" asked Veronica.

Tommy looked at her, smiling, "It had better, Doc, it had better."

An hour later they all left the brownstone, each heading to their agreed rendezvous points, preparing to act out the roles agreed upon.

Mac went back to the precinct as Graham Smithson, Junior had flown in late last and was calling at the station at 11 am. It seemed he had been out of the state on a business trip when his father Graham Smithson, Senior had been killed. Mac wanted to find out if the son could come up with any idea why his father would be killed and by whom? Strangely pattern-wise this murder was quite similar to the Jason Warrington one.

Doyle decided to revisit Mrs. Dean. One of the things missing from the Warrington Murder case files were details of the chauffeur. He wanted to see if she could come up with any more information. He asked Dutch, to take a photograph of Neil Parton to show his scammed ladies. He wanted to find out what their response was and if they recognised him.

As for Veronica, she was going to contact Mrs. Warrington, the daughter-in-law, and ask if she could call at the mortuary. She wanted her to bring in some old brushes of the late Mr. Warrington for forensic examination. If asked why, Veronica was to say that new evidence had come to light and they needed to recheck the DNA. It was in reality a ruse to get the lady away from the house so Mac could send a team in to search the chauffeur's residence. Mr. Warrington had already notified Mac he could be contacted at his office after ten o'clock. That meant they would only have the guard on the gate to contend with.

Later in the day, after they had all completed their tasks, the four of them met up at O' Malley's Bar for dinner. After eating, they strolled back to the brownstone to put what they had found into the case file and go over the final part of the plan. That night they all slept easily, being more relaxed than they had been for some days.

* * * * *

The next morning at 8.00 am Mac, Tommy and Dutch left for the precinct, while Veronica returned to the Mortuary to carry on her normal day job. She was disappointed that she couldn't be in on the final 'kill' but that wasn't her job. It had surprised her how much she had enjoyed being involved in the undercover work that Tommy and Mac did. Whilst that wasn't her expertise, she was still an integral part of any investigation, and shouldn't forget that.

Walking into the precinct, Smithy gave Mac the thumbs up, indicating that they had all the interested parties waiting to be interviewed. Entering his office, Doyle and Dutch following, Mac sat down and spread the files across the desk. Sitting down, he paused before speaking. "Okay, guys, this is it. It's now or never. Dutch you do understand that we get precedence with two murders over your scamming?" Dutch nodded his head. Whilst he wasn't one hundred percent happy, still it would be a result. Besides if it got the bastards of the streets, saving other women from being taken for a ride, then all well and good.

As for Tommy, all he was hoping for, was that the result would mean one of the very few unsolved open cases from his time on the job would be finally shut. Mac knew how important this was to Tommy and hoped that the result would be all his pal wanted it to be.

Finally, Mac stood and said, "Okay guys, let's get this show on the road. Sorry, Dutch I can't let you in on the interviews but you can watch from the backroom. Luckily, Tommy here is still commissioned to work for the force so he gets an exemption. Hope you understand?"

Dutch nodded. He had been involved far more than he expected, so couldn't complain. As long as he was there at the end, and the 'vic's' got their just deserts, he would be happy. "No problems, Mac. You've done right by me; by letting me be in on this so far. So, thanks."

Mac nodded, then turning to Doyle, he said, "Come on, Tommy, time for some fun." The men left the room and headed for the interview rooms.

They had decided to start with Edward Warrington. The man wasn't too pleased to have been kept sitting in a police waiting room for over four hours. He had been dragged from his bed at 7.00 am, with no excuse or reason given other than he was helping with their enquiries. What followed was not pleasant for Mr. Warrington. Despite his insistence that he knew nothing about his fathers' murder, it soon became apparent that Doyle had done his homework. The nail in the coffin, so to speak, was when Doyle showed him two photographs. One of his late father's chauffeur, who had mysteriously disappeared a few days after the murder, and one of their suspect, Neil Parton.

His responses had been, 'No comment,' until Mac suddenly produced a photo of a gun, asking, "Mr. Warrington, do you recognise this gun?"

"No comment."

"What would you say if I told you that we found this gun hidden on a secret shelf inside the chimney breast of the chauffeur's apartment at your home?" It appears that the Police thought they had originally missed it. However, we believe the chauffeur who worked for Mr. Warrington, Senior, placed it there after the Police search and before disappearing. What Mac didn't say, was that the stupid man hadn't bothered to wipe it clean.

"No comment. I would like to speak to my lawyer now," replied Edward.

Mac, acknowledging the man's request, terminated the interview and both he and Doyle left the room. Warrington, Junior was returned to a prison cell pending the arrival of his lawyer.

As they strolled down the corridor, Doyle said, "One down, three to go."

The next interview was with Graham Smithson, Junior. This strangely went along much the same lines as the Warrington one. Again, it concluded with Doyle showing the two photographs. With no response, Mac told Smithson that a team of police officers were, at that very moment, stripping the old ranch to pieces. He felt that if they could find evidence all these years after one murder, then why not after a more recent one. Smithson finally clammed up solid, so Mac had him thrown in a cell pending further enquiries. The man was not amused, nor was his legal beagle.

The next interview was with Neil Parton. As soon as Doyle and Mac entered the room, his legal beagle began demanding that his client be allowed to leave or he would complain to the Commissioner of Police. Mac told him to go ahead, he could leave now and complain but… his client was staying and would be interviewed. They did, after all, have a local brief on tap should he choose to go. The man changing his mind, decided on choosing to stay.

For most of the interview, Neil Parton acted cockily and arrogant. That was until Mac turned to Tommy, asking him, "Tommy, tell me when you went to see Mrs. Dean yesterday afternoon was she helpful?"

Doyle took his time in answering, "She was indeed, Mac. She gave me a positive ID. Said it was definitely him."

"Err... who is Mrs. Dean?" asked the legal beagle.

Mac nodded his head, indicating that Doyle could take the lead. "Well, Mrs. Dean was the housekeeper for the late Mr. Warrington. And do you know, when I showed her a photograph of Mr. Parton, she recognised him immediately? She told me all about him."

"What. I don't know any Mrs. Dean. She doesn't know me. It's a set-up," yelled Neil Parton.

Doyle and Mac sat back, a slightly smug look crossing their faces, while the legal beagle did his best to calm his client down. Once he was calmer, Doyle continued. "The thing is, it's true Mrs. Dean did recognise a picture of Mr. Parton. I believe you have a twin brother, don't you? The question is whether it was he or you who was the Warrington's chauffeur. We're not sure as he disappeared shortly after the murder. Doesn't matter really, as your face fits as much as your brothers does."

"What! I don't know what you're talking about. And if it was my brother, well, I ain't his keeper," snarled Neil Parton.

"No, that's true you aren't. But you are his partner in crime," said Mac and before Parton or his brief could respond he went on. "The thing is Neil, we could never find the gun that killed Mr. Warrington. Oh, we tried. We searched that house. Every last bit of it. And because Edward Warrington changed the layout of the place, we lost the whole crime scene."

Parton started to grin, but Mac wasn't done. He wanted to stretch the torture out so he could complete a 'fete an accompli' in style. Then he rethought his move. This was really Tommy's bag. It was his case – the one that nearly got away. Mac felt Tommy should be the one to cinch the deal. "Why don't you take it from here, Tommy. Explain to Mr. Parton exactly what we discovered this morning?"

Swallowing, a surprised Doyle picked up a report from the pile on the desk. Slowly he read it, nodding his head and pursing his lips. "Now, Neil. As Inspector Mackintosh has just explained, Mr. Edward Warrington did have some changes carried out to his late fathers' house. However, one of the things that are often difficult to change, is the structure or position of the chimney breasts. While he made changes in the main house, he couldn't be bothered doing so in the Chauffeurs' apartment. Did you know I was on Mr. Warrington's murder case? We searched every inch of that building, including the apartment. Well, you can imagine my surprise when, today, they rechecked the apartment and discovered, hidden up the chimney, a small package wrapped in a dirty rag?" Doyle paused, allowing his comments to take effect.

After waiting a few more minutes, it was Mac who continued explaining. "Well, I know I was gob-smacked. Do you know why, Neil? Because inside the rag was a gun," and Mac turned over the photo of the handgun, lying on a dirty rag. "And, do you know what was more surprising, Neil, was the fact that forensics have discovered that this was the very gun that killed Mr. Warrington. Now, the question is, if the gun wasn't there when we originally searched the building, how did we manage to find it today?"

No one spoke. Parton started swallowing and he looked to be getting a little edgy. He kept casting glances at his legal guy, but he just stared ahead, seemingly intrigued by what was being said. Finally, the lawyer spoke. "I'm sorry, Inspector, But I cannot see what this has to do with my client. As he has said he doesn't know Mrs. Dean or Mr. Warrington. And what his brother, if it is his brother, gets up to, is not within his control."

Mac smiled slightly. "Ahh… now that's where you are wrong Mr. Barnes. You see, as I said, what we did when we found the gun was to have it forensically examined. Do you know central heating is great. No lives fires in the chauffeurs apartment anymore! So, despite it having laid in the chimney for the last fifteen years, they were still able to get some decent prints from it." Mac paused, allowing that piece of juicy information to soak into Parton's head.

The reaction was all he could have expected; Parton turned white. "I'd… I'd... like to speak to my lawyer, now," he said.

"Sure," said Mac. "Interview suspended at…"

As they left the room, Doyle felt good. They were one step closer.

"What d'ya think, Tommy?" asked Mac, as they walked down the corridor.

Tommy laughed. "I think you're stretching it out. Giving him as much as you can, but not all at once." Mac looked at him. "Not that I'm complaining, Mac. Let's hope we can make the other one roll."

Leaving Neil Parton to stew, Mac and Tommy made their way to the interview room where Philip Parton sat waiting. Dutch joined them before they entered, saying, "Wow, you two guys are quite the thing, aren't you? No wonder you both made Inspector. I'm in awe," and they all laughed at the backhanded compliment.

"Ready for the next round, Dutch?" asked Mac.

"Bring it on, Mac, bring it on, this is way more interesting than in my day."

The interview techniques were much the same as with the other brother and when Mac asked Philip why he had disappeared so soon after the murder his answer was assured. "Family illness. I did tell the police before I left and they said it was okay."

After playing cat and mouse for about fifteen minutes, Doyle finally looked straight at Philip and told him how Mrs. Dean had recognised his brother's photograph. Then Mac told him about finding the gun. This time he told him it was being tested for fingerprints etc., and that at the moment it looked as if either he or his brother, or both of them, would be arrested for murder.

Finally, Mac said, "Oh! And by the way, we know all about the pair of you scamming women of their savings and jewellery. So, I'll tell you here and now, Philip, you're both going down. For how long though will depend on whichever one of you coughs up first. That's the one who will get first dabs at a deal. You think about it, Philip. Sentence for a double murder is double life?" And Mac stood up ready to leave the room.

Philip Parton had begun to shake. Then he started to cry. Mac stopped. "Got anything you want to say, Philip?"

His brief suggested he have a few moments with his client. Reluctantly Mac agreed, so he and Doyle left the room. Outside Tommy asked, "Do you think he'll roll?"

Mac shrugged his shoulders. "Hopefully."

Back in Mac's office, Dutch, Tommy, and Mac sat quietly discussing the interviews as they waited to see who would crack first. Doyle felt the Parton twins wouldn't give, but Mac disagreed thinking maybe Philip would give his brother up. Perhaps turning states evidence. What Mac really wanted was for them to implicate both Warrington and Smithson in each of their father's murders. Little did he know how much his wish was to come true.

Forty minutes later the first to agree to talk was Philip Parton. Entering the room alone, Doyle having agreed to Mac's request to sit it out, Mac sat down and recommenced the interview. Twenty minutes later it was all over. The dominoes were lined up and with a single push, they started falling. Fifteen years of history, two murders, and ten counts of embezzlement were solved in a flash. By six o'clock the three men, Doyle, Dutch, and Mac left the precinct feeling satisfied with the days' events.

* * * * *

Veronica walked into O'Malley's Bar around seven to find the three amigos drinking and laughing merrily. Looking up, Doyle's eyes met hers. It may have been the drink, but as he looked at her he found a sudden desire of wanting to kiss her.

"Hey, Doc, you made it?" called Mac. The moment for Doyle passed. Mac had given him the much-needed time to recover his equilibrium.

Smiling, Veronica, sauntered over to their table. "Well, gentlemen, I see you've started the celebrations without me."

Standing, Doyle said, "Sorry, Doc, what's your tipple?"

After getting her a drink, Veronica and Doyle returned to the table. The food they had already ordered arrived so conversation was lost in the enjoyment of eating and drinking. By the time the evening ended all four were as merry as hell, especially Doyle. Returning to the brownstone well after midnight the four finally crashed in their beds, enjoying a refreshing night's sleep.

* * * * *

The following morning Veronica was in the kitchen when Doyle finally surfaced. The smell of fresh brewing coffee having drawn him upstairs. "Good morning, Tommy. Boy did you lay one on last night," and she laughed lightly.

"Don't remind me, Doc," said Doyle, holding his head and wondering when the beating inside it would stop.

Veronica held out a glass of water with two Alka-seltzers' sizzling away inside. Doyle swallowed it down in one go. As she took the glass back, she handed him a mug of strong black coffee. Again, Doyle took a couple of swigs and felt the world returning to normal.

"Thanks. I needed that."

She laughed lightly again, then leaning forward she took his face in her hands and bending his head she lightly kissed his forehead. "There you go, Tommy, all better."

For a moment they looked into each other's eyes. Time stood still. Then slowly Tommy began moving forward. He had every intention of kissing her when suddenly the phone rang out.

Cringing, he screwed his eyes up, and turning away he grabbed the receiver, snarling, "Doyle."

Veronica had left before the call was finished.

THE WRAPPED PACKAGE

Doyle woke with a headache. Not caused this time, from a night out on the tiles. He'd been having headaches regularly. Something felt wrong. It wasn't like him to suffer like this. He had always been strong and healthy, passing his police medical and fitness tests each year without a problem. He must be getting old. As he sat drinking his second mug of black coffee, he realised that perhaps he'd not been as careful with his health since leaving the force as he should have. By his third cup of coffee, he had decided to take action. He would start jogging. And cut down on the beer. Well, it was a beginning.

Going down to the office, he searched on the internet for the type of clothing and footwear he should get, to look the part of a jogger. Finding what he wanted he left the brownstone and headed for the shopping mall. By the time he returned his headache had passed, and he was one hundred dollars lighter.

True to his decision, Doyle forewent the beer, although not that much of the coffee.

However, he woke the next morning with a clear head. Dressing in his new gear he set off gently running around the block. He had decided to start slowly, building up the speed and distance as he went on. Little did he realise how useful that would be to him in the very near future.

* * * * *

Mystery writer Gabriel Rodriguez was off to his studio. A small purpose-built office he rented in his publishers' building, in downtown Hollywood. Not the most salubrious of buildings or areas within the city, but certainly one of the cheapest opportunities. Besides, it got him out of the house he shared with his parents, his sister, and her two annoying children.

Each day, Gabriel, would catch the subway. And for a man whose life existed in the world of intrigue and adventure, albeit through his writing, nothing had ever happened to make his journey exciting or interesting. To help him concentrate on his plots and stories he always wore his earbuds, usually listening to either the music of Gershwin or one of the classics. An eclectic mix - but then he was a writer. His dress was always consisted of black pants matched with a hoodie. Gabriel was ignored, and he ignored in return.

That is until he was returning home one evening after a particularly stressful meeting with his publisher. So wrapped up was he in his own little world, thinking about the comments the publisher had made regarding his latest manuscript, that Gabriel was not paying attention to what was happening around him. As he walked along, he was suddenly startled out of his world when a frantic Middle-Eastern man, running as if the devil himself were after him, knocked him over and stunning him. Slowly picking himself up from the floor, Gabriel noticed the man racing down the stairs of the Metro. Following behind were several other mysterious-looking people. Gabriel brushed himself off, thinking, 'They must be rushing for the train?' before he carried on down the street, disappearing around the corner, and entering the shopping mall.

Deciding he needed a drink to settle his nerves, Gabriel looked for a bar. Tapping himself for his wallet, he suddenly felt a strange lump in the pocket of his hoodie. That hadn't been there before? Before the foreign man had bumped into him. Putting his hand gently inside the pocket he slowly withdrew the object. It was a small wrapped package. Looking around, in case someone was watching, he slid the package back inside. What was it? The man must have slipped it in when he bumped into him. Looking around surreptitiously, Gabriel didn't know what to do.

"What can I get you, Sir?" asked the waiter. Gabriel didn't reply. "Do you want to order or not?"

Looking up, Gabriel said, "Err... no thanks. My friends have been delayed so I'll... leave it thanks," and getting up he left the bar, heading for the opposite entrance to the one he had entered by.

What was he to do? Give it to the police? Perhaps it was valuable? There could be a reward? He could do with some luck, just now? Perhaps, he should keep it? No, keeping it would be stealing. The trouble was he didn't know who the strange man had been. How would he get in touch with him? Finally, Gabriel decided to take the package home. Once there he would check what was inside and then make a decision on what to do. Leaving the bar, he headed for the rear entrance of the shopping mall. He should take a taxi home. You never knew who might be around and he didn't want to lose his prize. At least before finding out what it was and whether it was worth some money.

Arriving home without incident, Gabriel went straight upstairs to his room to change out of his travelling clothes. He realised he couldn't carry the package around with him in the house, nor could he leave it just lying around. Too many inquisitive little eyes and fingers. Locking his door, he went into his bathroom, bending down he removed the cover at the base of the cabinet. Then carefully he prised open the loose floorboard hidden beneath the cabinet. Inside was a small metal box. Lifting it out he slipped the small package inside. Returning the box, he replaced both the floorboard and the cabinet cover. Everything looked normal. Anyone looking around would never guess he had a hidey-hole for his utmost secrets. Having changed he went downstairs and joined the noisy family for their evening meal.

* * * * *

The following morning Gabriel sat in his bedroom, listening to the news on his small radio. The kids had gone to school, his sister to work and his parents had left for their local church. Despite their insistence, Gabriel had refused to join them, explaining he had a lot of work to do and a deadline to meet. When his father started complaining about him missing church too often, Gabriel became annoyed, reminding him that if it wasn't for his work they couldn't live in the house, or in the style they did. It was time his father accepted that Gabriel's writing was God's way of showering his blessing on them. His father had left feeling disgruntled.

Now here he was, and for the first time in quite a while, he had the house to himself, plus some peace and quiet. Turning the radio up the newsreader came on announcing breaking news.

"The Police are looking for anyone who was in the area of the Gower Street Metro entrance, South Hollywood between the hours of seven and eight pm last night. This is following a shooting incident where a gentleman of Middle-Eastern origin was gunned down by a person or persons unknown. The Police say they are looking for at least four perpetrators who they believe were involved in the incident. If you were in the area, please contact Police on 747 91600"

Gabriel froze. He couldn't believe what he had just heard. What had happened? Was that the same man who had run into him? My God, what had he become involved in? Running into his bathroom he quickly removed the cabinet cover and floorboard. Lifting the metal box out, he slowly withdrew the package, still trying to decide what to do. Suddenly he realised he was shaking. Hell, what was he going to do? If those guys were after this, whatever it was, then they could come for him. He had to get rid of it. No! He had written enough thrillers to know, that even if he got rid of the package, they could still come for him. And his family. Replacing the package in the metal box and hiding it again, Gabriel went downstairs to think the situation over.

As he made himself a cup of coffee Gabriel noticed he was still shaking. Calming down and thinking over his situation, he finally decided he had to leave. Find somewhere else to live until the bad guys were caught. But where? He could go to the other side of LA. It was then he had a flash of brilliance. Tommy Doyle. He would go see him.

Gabriel had met Doyle a couple of years ago when he had been writing his last thriller, *'Dangerous Liaisons.'* He had asked Doyle for some tips about being a PI and how his protagonist would have gone about looking for and saving a bored wife from a dangerous guy. Doyle had been more than willing to help, giving him tips based on one of his real-life cases which he had given Gabriel permission to use; as long as he changed the names and places. This he had done. The book had won Gabriel an International Thriller Award, boosting his standing as a writer and, pleasing his publisher.

Searching through his desk, Gabriel found the business card Tommy had given him, then picking up the phone he dialled the number. The phone rang out, until a voice announced, "Doyle's Private Investigation. Sorry, I am currently out on a case, please leave your name and number and I'll get back to you asap." The answering machine bleep sounded and Gabriel started to leave a garbled message. Realising he wasn't making sense he slammed the phone down and ran up the stairs to get dressed.

About to put his usual pants and hoodie on, he changed his mind, choosing a suit and tie instead. If the guys chasing the dead man had seen him, they could recognise his clothing. Better to look different.

* * * * *

An hour later Gabriel tried the door of Doyle's brownstone but to no avail. Wondering what to do, he was about to leave when someone asked, "Are you looking for Tommy?"

Turning, Gabriel saw a lovely auburn-haired woman in her mid-thirties staring up at him. It was Janice Bartholomew, the accountant who lived next door to the Mini-Market.

"Erm… yes. I was hoping to find him in. I err… met him a couple of years ago and he helped me with a book I was writing. I'm hoping he can offer me some more advice," explained Gabriel.

Janice smiled. "Oh! You're Gabriel Rodriguez, the writer. I remember Tommy telling me all about you. I got your book when it came out. I loved it."

Gabriel was surprised. He didn't often come across many women who read his style of books. "You did, really? Thanks for buying it. Err… do you think Mr. Doyle will be back anytime soon?"

"Oh, yes. Mind you, sometimes he goes for a meal first. Down at O'Malley's Bar & Grill. You could try there."

Gabriel smiled. Janice seemed a nice lady. In fact, she was one of the very few women he had met that he was attracted to. "Mmm… I don't suppose you fancy joining me for a drink, do you? Sorry, I shouldn't have asked. You're probably married."

Janice smiled back. She liked what she saw. "Well, I have just finished work and I was going to get a sandwich, but... I could just as easily have one at the bar instead. So yes, if the offer still stands, I'd like a drink."

Happily, for the first time in a long time, Gabriel felt pleased he had taken the plunge and asked someone to join him. Well, for a drink anyway. Ten minutes later, they entered the Bar and finding a table in the corner, they ordered a sandwich and drink. After which they sat chatting about the various books Gabriel had written. As well as the other things they had in common, such as music, jogging, and films. So engrossed were they in each other that they almost missed Tommy when he entered the bar along with Mac.

Spotting Doyle, Janice called out, "Hey, Tommy, you have a visitor."

Doyle, turning to look saw Gabriel sat next to Janice. He crossed the room to join them. "Well, well, Gabriel, how you doing," he said. "It's been a while," and he held his hand out to shake the young man's hand.

"I'm very well, Mr. Doyle. I wondered if I could talk to you, please?"

Doyle smiled, "Sure, what about?"

Gabriel looked around surreptitiously before answering. "It's something personal, perhaps at your office when you're free?"

Doyle had noted the movement and wondered what was up, but rather than ask he merely said, "I'm going to grab a bite to eat. You finish your food and then we'll go back to the office together for coffee. It'll be quieter there," and smiling he rejoined Mac.

"Who's that," asked Mac.

"Remember me telling you about the writer guy who came to me a couple of years ago, well that's him," said Doyle.

Mac laughed, "Come to pick your brains again, has he?"

Doyle looked at Gabriel, before saying, "Actually, I think not. I have a feeling he's in trouble. Okay, Mac, let's eat." The subject was closed, as Doyle and Mac began discussing other more relevant matters while they ate.

Once lunch was over, Doyle said bye to Mac, and motioning to Gabriel he headed out of the Bar. A few seconds later the young man caught up with him. Together they strolled down the street to the brownstone that was Doyle's home and office. Once inside, and having made coffee, the pair sat down in Doyle's office where Gabriel explained all that had happened to him the previous day.

Doyle sat pondering the story he had just heard, a little surprised by the contents. Finally, he said, "And what's in the package?"

Gabriel looked shocked, answering, "I... err... haven't opened it! I daren't."

Doyle laughed. "Why the hell not. For all, you know it could be drugs. Come on, hand it over, let's have a look."

Gabriel was surprised. Hesitantly he took the small package from his pocket and reluctantly handed it across to Doyle. "Do you think we should do that? Open it, I mean?"

Doyle looked up. "Well, Gabriel, I need to know what the hell I am saving you from and why, don't I? So come on hand it over."

Taking the small package, Doyle laid it on the desk. Before opening it, he set up his video camera so he could record what he did and what was inside the package. Then with care, while explaining his movements, he began to undo the package. "I have received a small package of approximately five centimetres by five centimetres by six centimetres deep. The weight I guess to be approximately forty grams. The package consists of plastic fastened by grey sticky tape." Pausing, Doyle picked up a sharp stiletto blade and began talking again. "I am now gently slitting the edges of the tape and am carefully cutting through the plastic to create a small hole through which I can assess the contents of the package." Again, Doyle stopped talking whilst he concluded this action, ensuring the hole was big enough for him to extract a sample of the contents. "There appears to be something hard inside the package so I am concluding that the contents are not drugs. I am, therefore, now going to open the package fully and empty the contents onto the table."

Using the stiletto blade, Doyle cut two slits across the top of the package. Then he gently prised open the stiff sticky tape to reveal a small cloth bag. Removing all the packaging he started talking again. "It appears that the package contains a soft, blue velvet bag that feels to contain some small hard objects. I am guessing that these could well be stones of some description." Carefully opening the drawstring of the velvet bag Doyle slowly tipped the opened bag upside down and watched as a cascade of white stones fell onto the desk.

Both Doyle and Gabriel sat and stared in awe at the glorious crystal stones that glittered and shimmered in the glow from the desk lamp.

"Diamonds," whispered Gabriel starting to reach out to touch them.

"Stop. Don't touch them. Do not leave your imprint on them," snapped Doyle sharply.

Gabriel looked up in surprise, wondering why?

"Blood... These are conflict diamonds," announced Doyle. "Hell, Gabriel, what have you got yourself mixed up in?"

Suddenly Gabriel started to shiver. "Are, are, you sure, Mr. Doyle? I mean how do you know they're conflict diamonds?"

Doyle swallowed hard, before replying. "Past experience, Gabriel. I worked on a case a long time ago but you never forget what conflict diamonds look like. They have a unique appearance of their own. I need to get these to Mac and get you some protection.

Whoever they belong to is going to want to get them back."

Finding a pair of tweezers, Doyle carefully counted and replaced the diamonds into the velvet bag. There were twenty-five stones of varying sizes. "At an estimated guess this little lot must be worth at least thirty million dollars."

"What…!" gasped Gabriel. "You're joking? Do you think there'll be a reward for handing them in?"

Doyle looked at Gabriel, answering seriously, "Gabriel, the very fact you have these in your possession means certain death. These don't belong to the sort of people who advertise that they are missing, or who will offer a reward to the finder. These belong to people who will kill to get them back. No questions, no arguments, and certainly no negotiations for a reward. Got it?"

Seeing the look on Doyle's face, Gabriel suddenly realised just how deep in the shit he really was. And not just him. His family as well. He started to shake, wondering what he was going to do. "Yes, Mr. Doyle. I got it."

"Good. Right, let's go." Placing the velvet bag and the packaging in a plastic bag, Doyle stood up and headed for the door. "You coming or what?"

Gabriel looked up, then jumping to his feet he quickly followed Doyle. 'Hell,' he thought. 'What a bloody mess.'

* * * * *

Twenty minutes later Doyle walked into Mac's office with Gabriel trailing behind him.

Mac was surprised as Tommy didn't usually turn up unexpectedly. If he was here, then there was trouble brewing. "Tommy, what can I do for you," he asked as Doyle shut the office door. Now Mac knew something was seriously wrong. Tommy never shut the door without first asking.

Sitting down Doyle began explaining the problem. Taking the plastic bag out of his pocket he presented Mac with the diamonds, the packaging, and the videotape he had made of him opening the package. Having listened, Mac finally whistled. All he could say was, "Hell!"

"So, Mac, what do you think we should do?" asked Tommy.

Mac thought for a moment before answering. Then turning to Gabriel, he asked, "Do you think the guys who were chasing the one who ran into you got a good glimpse of you?"

Gabriel thought for a moment. "I honestly don't know. I don't think so. I had my normal jogging gear on – black pants and a hoodie. I usually wear the hood up and have my earbuds in. Didn't hear anything until the man ran into me and sent me flying. I didn't find the package until later when I called at a bar in the shopping mall. I needed something to calm me down. Had a bad meeting with my publisher so wasn't exactly concentrating and I was already upset anyway."

"I see," said Mac. He thought some more, wondering what would be the best way to proceed.

"I was thinking maybe some protection. Gabriel does have a family; parents, a sister, and she has kids. Perhaps send them away for a while? Gabriel touched the outside but only I have touched the inside and then only the bag. The diamonds I picked up with tweezers as you'll see from the video," explained Tommy.

Mac pondered a bit more. Finally, he said, "I agree. We need to get Gabriel and his family away. Even though he can't ID the perps they don't know that. Or that he's given us the diamonds. Okay. Tommy, can you take Gabriel back to your place for now? I'll speak to the Commissioner and get something rolling asap. I'll also put a couple of patrol cars around Gabriel's home area, just in case."

Standing Doyle agreed to do as Mac had asked. "Come on, Gabriel, let's get back. You can ring your dad once we get back and tell him you're in a meeting for the rest of the day. No need to worry them just yet. See you later, Mac," and he headed for the door.

"Get back to you, asap, Tommy. Watch your back, pal?"

* * * * *

Back at the brownstone, Doyle told Gabriel to settle in while he went to the office to do some research. He wanted to try and find out who the guys chasing the murdered man might have been. He needed to chat to a couple of his informers. By the time he returned to the upstairs apartment Tommy had learned that some new middle eastern guys were hanging around the district. Out-of-towners, his informant had told him. Mean and nasty. They were mixing with a few of the Somalians who had recently come to the downtown district. It was rumoured the out-of-towners had gone after the dead guy because he'd cheated the Somalians on a deal. Tommy knew that would interest Mac; and not just him but Homeland Security as well.

Two hours later, Mac arrived accompanied by a couple of 'suit jobs' – in other words, Homeland Security. Tommy was not overly pleased. The last time he had encountered these guys it had not ended well; almost costing him his life.

As they entered, Mac threw Tommy an apologetic look – it didn't help ease the tension which you could have cut with a knife. "This is Special Agent Thomas and Dixon. They would like to speak to Gabriel, Tommy. Okay."

"Would it make any difference, if I said it wasn't?"

"Hell, Doyle, don't you ever forgive and forget," snarled Agent Thomas.

Doyle didn't answer the man. Instead, he looked at Mac and said, "Gabriel is upstairs. But, if you think I am going to let him go with these two, you can think again. He's breathing now and I expect him to continue doing so. You can show them the way," and turning away he headed for his office.

An hour later, Mac knocked on the office door, waving a white hanky around it. "Is it safe to come in?"

Looking up, Tommy had to laugh. "Yea, as long as you are on your own and the sons of Satan have left – minus Gabriel?"

Mac smiled. There were times when Doyle had a way with words. "They've returned to hell, minus their witness, who couldn't help them. And, who refused flat out to leave this heavenly sanctuary of yours." They both burst out laughing.

Once calmer, Doyle apologised for his attitude regarding his welcome of the two Agents but Mac waved it aside, saying, "Hell, I don't blame you, Tommy. After what happened, I'm surprised you didn't smack him."

Tommy laughed again, finally saying, "I did – the last time I met him, I laid him out. Got escorted out of an event by the Commissioner who read me the riot act while doing it. Once out of sight he shook my hand warmly and told me well done, and if anyone asked, I got three days suspension. Off the record, my slate was clean."

Mac laughed. Shaking his head, he declared, "Well done, mate, well done."

As calm reined once more, Tommy asked what was going to happen next. Sitting down with a fresh mug of coffee, Mac brought him up to speed. "First thing, is to get Gabriel's family out of the house and away. Gabriel says they can go stay with some relatives' upcountry. Next is to decide what to do with Gabriel. We can keep him under lock and key but if they want their diamonds back, they arc going to come looking for him. I have a plan. I'll need your help but… it's a bit dangerous. From what I can gather these guys don't play by the rules. The idea is to be able to draw them out and catch them in the act so to speak. It's up to you, Tommy?"

Before answering, Tommy took a swig off his coffee, savouring the taste and the small burning sensation it provoked on his tongue. "Hell, yes. Of course, I'm in. Tell me what you want?" After which he and Mac spent the next hour going over their plan of action for catching the murderers and hopefully, the importers of the diamonds.

* * * * *

"Why do we have to leave our home?" yelled Gabriel's father. "This is all your fault. You got us into this mess. You and your stupid writing."

Gabriel sighed. He was beginning to get exasperated by his fathers' reactions to Mac's demands that the family leave their home and go to stay somewhere safe out of town. Before he could speak, Doyle stepped forward.

"Mr. Rodriguez, as we've already explained, it was by sheer chance that Gabriel was knocked down by the murdered victim. He wasn't to know that the man had slipped the diamonds into his pocket, now was he. All we want you to do, is to go somewhere you will be safe until we capture the culprits who killed the man, and who are probably looking for your son. We don't want to see you or your family get hurt."

"It's just a precaution, Sir," concluded Mac. "Better safe than sorry."

Mr. Rodrigues, Senior was still not happy at having to uninstall himself, his wife, daughter, and two grandchildren from their home. Nor with the fact that Doyle and a couple of police officers would be moving in while they were gone. To him, his son was a stupid boy. "You should have got a proper job," he told Gabriel.

"In which case, we would still be living in that run-down place you liked so much," snapped Gabriel. "You seem to forget, it's my earnings from the writing that has put a roof and four good walls around the family, not yours." Unable to take any more of his father's nonsense Gabriel stormed out of the room, running upstairs to his bedroom and slamming the door with such force that the house almost shook with fright.

"Come, come, my dear," said the gentle voice of Mrs. Rodriguez. "I'm sure Gabriel didn't do it on purpose. Now, stop arguing and do as the nice policeman has requested." Then turning to look at Mac she asked, "You will take care of the house, won't you?"

Mac smiled and taking her hand he told her that they would treat all of her lovely possessions as if they were the Crown Jewels of England. Reassured by his warm smile, she took hold of her husband's hand and led him towards the door.

Later, once the Rodriguez family had left, and Doyle and the officers who would be staying to guard

Gabriel had settled in, Mac called a meeting. He wanted to set some ground rules, particularly for Gabriel. The last thing he needed was to put his prize witness in unnecessary danger. That done, the rest of the evening was spent in relative quiet.

* * * * *

The following morning when Gabriel came downstairs, he found Doyle sat in the kitchen drinking coffee. He was dressed in jogging clothes and trainers, as if ready for a run.

"Morning, Gabriel. Sleep, okay?"

"So, so, Mr. Doyle, and you?"

"Just fine. Okay, today I want you to go about your normal day. I will leave the house five minutes before you and will be waiting to pick you up when you reach the end of the road. The guys on duty in the car outside will watch you to the end of the street. I'll jog along behind you. Not too close – but close enough if needed. Okay?"

Gabriel nodded. He was beginning to feel nervous. The plan was he would go about his normal routine, wearing his usual black pants and hoodie. Mac had explained to him that there would be plain-clothes police all along the route, with Doyle following at a distance. He was to act the same as usual. Go to his office at the publishers and stay there as normal. Again, there would be officers following his every move. The Police Technician had placed a tracker in his phone just in case, and they had given him a whistle in case of emergencies. At the end of the day, he would return the same way home that he always did.

Despite all the precautions Gabriel was still extremely nervous when it came to time to step outside the house. As he hesitated the officer stood close by said, "Don't worry. We are watching you. And besides, you have Doyle. Couldn't get a better man covering your back. Okay?" Gabriel nodded, feeling some slight reassurance. Then taking a breath he left the house.

Following his usual routine, Gabriel jogged down the street and turned the corner. As he did, he caught sight of Doyle, bending down tying a shoelace. He jogged on past without looking. As soon as Gabriel was past him Doyle stood up, surreptitiously casting his eye around for any strangers who might be lurking about. Also checking that the undercover officers were in place. He then followed Gabriel at a safe but reasonable distance, always keeping him in his eyesight.

By the time they arrived at Gabriel's office, Doyle was satisfied that no one untoward had been following. Doyle kept on jogging, turning the corner at the end of the street and not stopping until he reached the entrance into the shopping mall. If he was wrong and he had been followed he would lose them inside the mall. As it happened this morning he wasn't followed. As for Gabriel. There was a couple of plain clothes officers situated inside the building who would now take over watching him. Doyle would return later when Gabriel was ready to leave.

The day passed by slowly. Doyle returned to the brownstone to do some more research. He was hoping he could come up with some further details about the illegal diamond trade. This he would share with Mac when they met up later.

At five o'clock as Gabriel left his office building, Doyle was ready to run around the corner and follow him. Again, at a safe distance, while keeping him in clear sight. The run home was clear and straightforward.

To say the guys involved were disappointed, was an understatement. But, as Mac told them, "There is time yet, so stay on guard."

This daily routine continued for the next few days. Nothing out of the ordinary. No strangers in the area. Nothing or no one near the metro entrance causing any concern. That was until the evening of the fourth day when all hell broke loose!

* * * * *

The journey out to Gabriel's office had gone as normal. Or so everyone thought. Everyone but Doyle. He had started to feel his nose twitching. It had become a joke in the precinct how Tommy's nose always twitched when there was trouble brewing. The more it twitched – the more trouble there would be. And today, Doyle's nose made him feel like Samantha from the TV show Bewitched. He needed to ring Mac and put them on high alert.

Now anyone else would have laughed and told Doyle to get lost. But not Mac. He knew Doyle. And if he said things were brewing? Then things were brewing. Leaving the precinct, he called for backup and headed out.

Gabriel left the office, stopping in the doorway for a moment. It was as if he sensed that something wasn't quite right. Maybe it was a second sense. Whatever it was he became wary. Looking around for Doyle, he spotted him tying his shoelace a little further up the street. Feeling reassured he set off towards the metro.

As Gabriel got closer to the Metro steps, he became aware of a couple of guys, dressed in dark clothes, hanging around close to the steps. They appeared to be watching him. Gabriel was wondering whether to cross the street, but looking across to the opposite pathway he noticed two more men, dressed similarly.

Slowing his footsteps, he took the whistle from his pocket and placed it into his mouth. Trying his best not to make eye contact with either of the two men, he prepared himself. Just as he got close enough for the two men to try and make a grab at him, he started to blow.

Doyle came rushing past, pushing him aside. He then barged into the two men with such force that he sent them both stumbling backward toward the Metro entrance. As he did, two offices from a parked car raced across the street. One went after one of the guys who had fallen down the steps of the Metro, while the other helped Doyle catch the second guy.

At the same time, four police officers had piled out of an unmarked police van close to where the other two villains were stood, and before they could do anything they were overpowered and arrested.

As all four were bundled into the Police paddy wagon which had just arrived, Doyle gently reached across to Gabriel. "You can stop blowing now, Gabriel," Doyle told him.

Gabriel was shaking so much, it took him a moment or two before he did as requested. "Is it over?" he whispered.

Doyle stood laughing, "Yes, Gabriel. It's over. At least for now. Come on, why don't we go into the shopping mall and get a drink. I think we could both do with one?" And leading the way, the pair headed for the High Five Bar situated just inside the shopping mall entrance.

They only returned to Gabriel's home, two beers and Bourbon shot later. Arriving back at the house, they found Mac waiting for them. "So, you two seem to be in good spirits."

Doyle laughed, "We are. Purely for medicinal purposes, Mac. Gabriel needed it after the day he's had." Both Mac and Gabriel laughed.

Finally, Gabriel asked, "What happens now, Inspector?"

"Well, I need you to try and do a line-up for me if possible? Do you think you might recognise any of the four we arrested? Would be great if you could."

Gabriel didn't answer straight away. Then having thought about it, he said, "I didn't recognise the faces but I did recognise the tattoos on their hands. The bigger guy leaning against the wall had a bar across his hand and spikes leading down to his fingers. The other guy also had a tattoo around his wrist. I can draw them for you if you like?"

"Hell, Gabriel. Why didn't you tell us this before?" said Doyle.

"Because I forgot. It was the shock of what happened that day. And then today it brought it all back. I'm sorry, Mr. Doyle," replied Gabriel sheepishly.

Mac smiled, saying. "That's okay, Gabriel. These things happen. But it will be a big help in nailing those two. Not that they are going anywhere. Appears the four of them are wanted in another state. Looks like our DA is going to have a fight on his hands trying to keep them here. They killed a whole family – seven people. Anyway, that's not my problem. I just catch the bastards."

Hearing Mac's words about the killing of the family shocked Gabriel. But it also meant that when his father came home, he could tell him how lucky he was to be alive. Not that he would see it that way. Perhaps it was time he moved out. Found his own place to live. At least then what ever happened to him wouldn't affect the family. Ahh well, that was for another day. For now, he needed a good night's sleep.

Doyle gathered his belongings and saying bye he got ready to follow Mac out of the door. They would leave a couple of officers in the house for now until things were settled and the villains had been removed upcountry. Once they were out of the state things would go back to normal for the Rodriguez family.

Mac was about to leave but stopped, turning back towards Gabriel, he said, "That family that was killed. They had already killed the son. He had been an accidental witness to the men committing a crime. He did a good deed by telling the police; he was a good citizen. Saved a girl's life. Did it all innocently. After his death, they still killed his family; even though he hadn't seen them for five years. Tell your father, that even if you hadn't lived here, those guys might still have come for him and the rest of the family. For me, you're a hero and you did the right thing. See you at the precinct tomorrow with the drawings. Good-night," and Mac left.

As Mac and Doyle walked along the street to the parked car, Doyle asked, "Was that bullshit, Mac?"

"Not quite. But it was close enough to give Gabriel something to put his old man in his place. My old man was like him. Everybody was in the wrong but him. Should have seen his face the day I told him I was a copper. He nearly turned puce," and Mac laughed at the memory.

Doyle smiled. "I would have thought he would be proud of you for achieving something. My mom was."

"True. Yea, you would have thought so. The problem was, Tommy, my old man was an ex-con. Supposed to be going straight, but I reckoned he never would. I thought if I became a copper, it would put him back on the straight and narrow and keep him there."

"And did it?" asked Doyle. Having never heard much about Mac's family he was curious.

Mac laughed. "Hell, no. He lasted about a month. Then I moved out; shared with another on the beat. Two weeks later I arrested the bastard for breaking into a jeweller's shop. Sixth offence for robbery. He got sent down for fifteen years. He was still on parole from his last job. Had a fall in prison and died. Good riddance to bad rubbish, I say. God rest his evil soul. Come on, Tommy, let's go eat. I need some of Molly O'Malley's cooking, and a good night on the booze."

Doyle smiled. He knew that feeling well.

WHERE'S THE GROOM

"Morning, Tommy." It was Jake the postman. He was stood at the bottom of the steps of the brownstone holding Doyle's mail in his hand. "You coming or going?"

Doyle laughed. "Popping to the Mini Market for some bread. Seems I ran out and forgot to shop. That my mail, Jake?"

"Sure is. Mmm... a fancy envelope," says Jake as he smells it. "Mmm... must be from a lady," and laughing he passed the mail across to Doyle.

Laughing in response, Doyle says, "I wish, Jake. Footloose and fancy-free, I am." Taking the envelope, he quickly tore it open, pulling out the contents. It was a wedding invitation. "Well, I'll be damned. It's from an old buddy of mine. Seems, his daughter, my god-daughter, is getting married. Hell, she can't be that old. She was only knee-high to a grasshopper the last time I saw her."

"They soon grow up, Tommy. My Julie will be fifteen in three weeks. Might need you one day to chase the boys off, for me," and laughing Jake headed away down the street, calling out, "Have a good one, Tommy."

"You too, Jake." Doyle laughed to himself at the postman's sense of humour. He had to admit that he was glad he wasn't a father. Well, at least not the father of girls. 'Mind you,' he thought. 'Not sure I would want boys either, these days.' And smiling he headed for the Mini Market.

* * * * *

Later that day, Doyle walked into Mac's – Chief Inspector Pete Mackintosh's – office at the local precinct. "Morning, Mac. Not reporting for duty, as requested," and he laughed.

Looking up, Mac smiled. "Very funny. You do realise what a lucky so and so you are. You don't have to get up until you want. No working all hours. No writing bloody reports. And, no answering to the bloody new Commissioner."

"Oops... what's he done now?"

Mac shook his head in disgust. "Only decided he wants to shake up the force. Reassess our working modus operandi. In other words, screw the system up. Meaning more work and fewer results."

Doyle started laughing loudly. Mac looked at him in disgust. "It's not bloody funny," he said indignantly. But once started, Doyle couldn't stop. Until slowly Mac let his indignation slide, and before long the pair of them were literally rolling in their seats in fits of uncontrolled laughter. "Bastard," said Mac looking at Doyle. But this only caused Doyle to laugh even harder, which in turn made Mac also laugh louder.

After about ten minutes or so, peace and calm reigned once more in the office. "Boy, Mac, you make my day. Retire. Get out. You've done enough. Take your pension and run for the hills."

Mac looked at Doyle seriously. "Don't bloody tempt me. At this precise moment, I'm tempted to join you in your game," and he laughed. "Out of the frying pan into the fire!"

Doyle laughed again and standing he said, "Come on, Mac, lunch is on me."

Leaving the building they crossed the road, going down the street where they stopped at The Hideout, a small café cum takeaway coffee shop. Ordering a sandwich and coffee the pair found a quiet table in the corner where they sat and ate in peace and quiet. Once settled, Doyle asked, "Honestly, Mac, are you that cheesed off?"

"Cheesed is not the word I would use. The new Commissioner has come in all guns blazing. He hasn't got a frigging clue what he's doing but he wants to make a big impression on the governor." Mac sighed, took a swig of the fresh brew of coffee, and then continued, "Seriously, Tommy, I've had it. I've worked damn hard to get to be Chief and now I just feel as if it's not been worth all the effort," and he sighed again.

Doyle nodded his head, sagely. He knew exactly what Mac was feeling but he wasn't sure how he could help his pal cope with this. A new Commissioner meant he, himself, would be out of the scene. The new guy wouldn't sanction any interference from an outsider, even if he was a decorated ex-cop. "What do you think you'll do?"

Mac didn't answer straight away, just sat in his seat thinking about it. Finally, he said, "Retire, Tommy. I'm going to retire." Doyle was shocked by the sudden announcement. Mac loved the job, as much if not more so than he had, so he knew how hard it was for him to have made such a decision.

"You sure, Mac. That's a big decision. Maybe the guy will realise he can't do what he says he wants and back off?"

Looking at Doyle, Mac said, "Too late, he's already started and there's going to be trouble in the ranks. I've already got six requests for transfers to other divisions. If he carries on the way he is, there won't be no police force in this area." And he sighed again, continuing with, "No, my mind's made up. I'm getting out while I can. I have a full pension, enough money saved, and with the offer I've had on the uptown apartment, I can afford to move upcountry and relax. Maybe open a small carpentry business. Perhaps, in Twin Peaks. It's a lovely place you have up there, Tommy. I'll be able to afford a small house and a business."

"Wow! I didn't know you were that well off," laughed Doyle.

"Hey, come on, Tommy, remember, no wife, working all hours, invested parent's money into property, nothing to spend my earnings on, so I have a tidy sum put away. And with the pension, well, I'm settled for the rest of my days. Small business to keep me occupied. You never know – I might meet and marry a nice rich widow up there," and they both laughed at the mere suggestion.

Lunch finished on a high note. Mac returned to his office, while Doyle went to the Morgue. He had had an idea about the Wedding Invitation and wanted to see the M.E., Dr. Veronica Martin. He knew she had the hots for him. So, if he was going to go to a wedding well, maybe she'd like to go with him. More fun than taking Mac!" The idea made him chuckle.

Knocking on the mortuary door, Doyle pushed it open slightly, and introduced himself through the small opening. "Anyone in?"

"Tommy Doyle is that you," called out the soft sultry voice of Veronica Martin, the Medical Examiner. "Come on in?"

Doyle entered the sterile domain of the mortuary, seeing Veronica removing her gloves, mask, and apron, having just finished her latest autopsy. The body had been quickly covered and was now being wheeled away by the medical assistant towards the refrigerated doors across the other side of the room. Even in her medical attire Veronica looked desirable, thought Doyle.

"And what can I do for you, Tommy?"

"I was passing and came for a chat, Doc. You free for a coffee?"

"Of course. Give me five minutes. I'll meet you in the small canteen down the hall."

Doyle nodded and left the room. If he was honest he was always glad to leave. That was one place he had no desire to be in... ever!

True to her word, Veronica joined Doyle five minutes later. She picked up the cup of coffee he had bought for her, took a couple of mouthfuls, and after swallowing, said, "Boy, did I need that."

"Heavy day, Doc?"

"Don't ask, Tommy." Then leaning across, in a conspiratorial voice she said, "Have you heard about the new Commissioner?"

Doyle nodded, asking, "Not you as well?"

"Too bloody true, me as well. Why can't a man, who knows nothing at all about a subject, just keep his hands to himself? Do you know what he did? He only came down into the mortuary and started telling me how to do my job. ME!" Veronica looked mortified. "Who the hell did he think he was... Quincy, M.E.? The only medical experience that man has had is by having a brush stuck up his behind."

At this comment, Doyle couldn't hold back any longer, as he suddenly burst out laughing. He laughed so much his sides hurt. However, it at least lifted the anger from Veronica as she too now saw the funny side of what she had just said. "Oh, Veronica. You've made my day, you really have," laughed Doyle, leaning over and kissing her on the cheek.

"Well, it was worth it, for the kiss," and leaning towards him she kissed him back.

A little surprised by her actions, Doyle didn't react. "You sound to have it as bad as Mac?"

She nodded her head, saying, "I am so bloody annoyed by that man, I could spit. But that would be unladylike and unclean in this place. He's a moron," and she smiled. "So, Tommy, what did you want to see me about?"

Although at first hesitating, 'Strike while the iron is hot,' Doyle told himself. Taking a breath he took the wedding invitation from his pocket and passed it across to her. "I've got this and... and, err... I wondered if you'd like to go with me?"

Taking the card, Veronica read it. Then looking up at Tommy, she asked, "What about, Mac?"

Doyle smiled. "Not quite sure it's his kind of thing. And I'm not sure I want to go on my own. I'd feel a bit of a gooseberry without someone. Preferably have a lady by my side. If you're not free that's okay. I'll probably just decline. But I thought I'd ask."

She looked at the date on the card, checked the diary she always carried with her, and then smiling said, "I would love to come with you. Thank you."

Doyle didn't answer straight away being in shock that she had said yes. Then quickly standing, he took the card back, saying, "Thanks. I'll ring you with details of what time I'll be picking you up. Oh. And, err... bring an overnight bag. I'll book us a couple of rooms. Means we can both have a drink. Catch you later," and with that, he was gone.

* * * * *

Two weeks later, Doyle pulled up outside the small house that was Veronica's home. It was situated in a quiet district, inside a secure gated community. The guard had had to ring through to get permission for Doyle to enter. By the time he pulled up outside her house, Veronica was stood waiting on the doorstep with her overnight bag.

As he climbed out of the car, which had been freshly washed and polished, Veronica noted how

121

smart Doyle looked. He was wearing a charcoal grey suit with a pale lavender dress shirt and a purple bow tie. His shoes were grey to match, and he had recently had his hair cut. There was a pale lavender kerchief in the top pocket of the jacket. If it hadn't been unladylike to whistle, Veronica would have given him the full salute.

The most surprising thing was, his outfit complimented her shaded pink and lilac two-piece dress outfit, with matching shoes. On her head, she wore a fascinator in similar colours that matched and blended well with her outfit.

Approaching the house, Doyle didn't resist the inclination to whistle, letting out a long slow one, and then saying, "Boy, do you scrub up great, Doc."

"I hope you aren't going to refer to me as – Doc – all day, Tommy?"

Smiling, he picked up her case, and as he turned away, he cheekily said, "Oh, no. I can think of lots of other very nice things to call you. But... some of them are for your ears only. Don't forget to lock up... sweetie!" And he laughed as he put her night bag in the boot of the car.

Leaving the complex, they headed for the motorway. The wedding venue was only a couple of hour's drive away, but Doyle wanted to make sure they missed the lunchtime traffic.

"By the way, Veronica, there's a button-hole each sat on the back seat. And, also a present. I've put your name to it along with mine. Hope you don't mind?"

Veronica was surprised. She hadn't given the idea of a gift any thought so was pleased Tommy had. "Err... what is it? Just so I know?"

"It's a barbeque set. There's a barbie to go with it as well. That's in the boot. I asked my mate what they wanted and his daughter chose a barbie. I bought the set as well. It looked good so thought they might as well have it. What do you think? Good enough?"

"That's great. If that's what they wanted then you've done good, Tommy."

Doyle smiled. He was feeling happy. Today was going to be a good day, even if it brought back a few bitter-sweet memories of his own wedding day. However, those would soon disappear with the doc, Veronica, by his side. Suddenly, life felt good to him.

* * * * *

Arriving at the hotel where they would be staying, Doyle checked them into their room. Then taking Veronica's hand he led her out of the side entrance, across the car park, and through the gateway into the wedding venue's car-park next door.

"Wow, now that's organisation for you," she laughed.

"Well, seeing those high heels of yours, if you get too drunk and I have to carry you back I won't have far to carry you will I?" laughed Doyle. Playfully, she hit him, but still laughed along with him. "Oh! By the way. There is one other thing I forgot to tell you. Macy, the bride, she's my god-daughter."

Before Veronica could respond a voice said, "Tommy, you old dog! About time you showed up."

As Doyle looked towards the sound of the voice he found a small group of men gathered together. All were police officers. "Grazie, how you doing, man?" said Doyle, holding his hand out.

"Hey, I'm good, how's you? Hey, do ya remember these reprobates?"

"Fine man, just fine. And yea, who could forget such a troublesome, rowdy lot," and before he knew it, Doyle was surrounded by the group of men, all greeting and patting him on the back, as well as playfully pretending to punch him.

Suddenly remembering the doc, he stepped aside, saying, "Hey, guys, I'd like you to meet a friend of mine. This is Veronica... Veronica Martin. Veronica, these are some of the guys I used to work with when I first joined the force."

"Well, hello boys. It's a pleasure to meet you. Perhaps you can tell me some of Tommy's secrets?" Her sultry, sexy voice, left all the guys with their mouths open for a moment.

"Yeah. Yeah sure, what do you want to know? We got alllll... the dirt on him."

"Hell, don't you bloody dare." And they all laughed at Doyle's discomfort. Then turning towards Veronica he pointed a finger at her in warning, "You will pay for that, madam," and he laughed at her as she stuck her tongue out.

"Okay, okay you lot, time to get inside the church. And that includes you, Thomas Doyle."

Everyone stopped laughing, saying 'yes ma'am' as they started heading towards the church door. Doyle grinned, as he looked down into the eyes of Martha Cresswell. There was only one woman who had ever called him Thomas, and this was she. His mate Patrick's, mother. She must have been ninety if she was a day. Placing his arms around her, he said, "And how is the most beautiful woman I know?"

She slapped him on his arm, giggled, and said, "Tosh. You always were a smooth one, Thomas. Kiss me, introduce this gorgeous young woman, and then get yourself inside that church. You hear me?"

"Yes, ma'am," he replied kissing her. "This is Veronica Martin, a special friend. Veronica this Granny Martha, my friend Patrick's mother, and the only lady to win my heart," whereupon he laughed and Martha slapped him again.

"And if you believe that tosh you'll believe anything. I'm pleased to meet you. Come on let's get inside the church? Macy is on her way," and taking Doyle's arm she began walking towards the church door. As she went, she whispered, "Very nice, Thomas, very nice. Better than the last one." Doyle couldn't find anything to say in return so thought it better to stay silent.

* * * * *

The wedding service was over and all the guests were making their way across the car park to the hotel, where the reception was being held in the large ballroom. Along the way, Veronica was introduced to some more of Doyle's old friends. Surprisingly, he held on tight to her hand all the way. Once inside the ballroom, they checked the seating chart and quickly found their table. As it happened they were sat with a few of Doyle's old buddies and their wives. After the introductions had been made, with everyone welcoming her, she and them seemed to relax meaning the rest of the day went with a swing. As the evening started to roll in, jackets were removed and people moved into the bars or went to their rooms to change. This was to allow the staff time to prepare the ballroom for the evening event.

Taking hold of her hand, Doyle said, "Do you fancy a walk?"

"Only if I can change my shoes, ha-ha?"

"No need, I wasn't thinking of going far. How about a short stroll in the garden?"

"Lead on, Sir," and she smiled at him warmly.

Finding the entrance into the garden at the rear of the hotel, Doyle suddenly swept her up into his arms and carried across the grass to a small alcove, near some trees. Standing her down he took a clean handkerchief from his trouser pocket and placed it on the wooden bench beneath the trees. "Your seat, madam."

Smiling, Veronica said, "Why thank you, kind Sir," and she sat down. Doyle joined her.

They sat in companionable silence, enjoying the peace of the early evening sun. After a while, he casually placed his arm around her. "You okay," he asked. "They haven't frightened you off, have they?" and he laughed.

"Yes, I'm okay. And no, Tommy, they haven't frightened me off."

Relaxing, he said nothing. Although the silence stretched, it was a comfortable silence. One in which they both felt at ease. Finally, Doyle said, "Veronica, are you serious about quitting your job?"

Surprised, she wasn't sure what to say. She had seriously been considering calling it quits but if she did... what next? There was nothing to stop her? Although, for a start, she would miss what she did. Okay, not as much as she thought. No. She would miss him. Doyle. If she gave up her job, then she wouldn't see him. There would be no reason to. Hell, was he playing a game with her? Oh my. It was like playing cat and mouse. The question was – who is the cat and who is the mouse.

Finally, she replied, "To be honest, Tommy, I'm not sure. If I quit what would I do. I suppose I could write that book I've been telling myself I want to do. But what if I can't write? What do I do then?" and her voice trailed off. She wondered if she had said too much.

"You know, the strange thing is, Mac was talking the same way. He's on about retiring. Opening a small carpentry business or some such thing in Twin Peaks. The funny thing is I've been thinking the same... Not opening a business, just retiring. I have the house. It could do with some refurbishment so that would occupy me. And then there's the garden. But I was thinking about how big it is... the house. It really needs a..."

"There you are, Tommy. I haven't had a chance to chat with you all day. Sorry... I'm not interrupting, am I? It's just that I need to talk to you."

"Err... no, that's okay, Patrick, is something up?" Doyle asked nicely, even though he was feeling annoyed at the interruption.

Veronica stood up. "I think I'll go to my room and refresh myself. Leave you two boys to have a nice chat." As Doyle stood, she pecked him on the cheek, smiled, patted his chest, and walked across the grass to the path as if she was floating. Doyle watched her, wondering.

"She's a looker, Tommy. Seems a nice lady."

"She is, Patrick. She's our local M.E. and I quite like her."

Laughing, Patrick said, "Like her? Tommy, you've got the hots for her. Take it from a man who knows. Strike while the iron's hot. You ain't getting any younger."

"Geez... thanks, Pat. You know how to boost a guy's morale, don't you? SO, what's the problem?"

Lowering his voice, Patrick said, "I think my son-in-law is in trouble? The problem is he won't speak to me. Keeps saying everything is okay. He can sort it. Err... I wondered if perhaps, you could... maybe have a few words with him. See if you can get some info, please?"

"Yea, of course I will. Better leave it till tomorrow though. Get today over with. I'll stay over a bit longer. Use the excuse I'm gonna show

Veronica my old patch. Let's talk tomorrow afternoon. Okay?"

Standing, Patrick wiped a tear from the corner of his eye. "Thanks, Tommy. You're a good 'un. Knew I could count on you. Thanks, pal," and he held his hand out for Doyle to shake.

After Patrick had left, Doyle sat pondering about what he had said. Finally, he stood thinking he'd better go and break the news to Veronica. If she chose not to stay then he'd pay for her to get a taxi back. For some reason, he hoped she wouldn't go.

* * * * *

Returning to the ballroom, Doyle found Veronica talking to Martha Cresswell. He stood watching her, wondering if he was too old to start walking the romantic pathway again. And yet, he thought why not. Looking up, Veronica caught him watching her. She smiled and he responded, before slowly crossing the room to join her.

Bending to kiss Martha, he said, "Do you fancy dancing with your toyboy, Martha?"

Looking up at him she almost blushed. "And who says you're my toyboy, Thomas Doyle?"

Pulling a face as if he was hurt, he said, "You did. So, fancy a dance?"

Smiling she stood up. Taking hold of her arm he led her onto the dance floor. The DJ put something smoochy on. Doyle gently took Martha in his arms and slowly waltzed her around the room. Everyone cheered and clapped. Calling out their names.

Veronica was amazed at Doyle's care and consideration for the old lady.

"Bet that's surprised you, hasn't it?" said Grazie. Veronica nodded her head.

"It's a sort of tradition. Ever since Tommy became part of the family. He moved in with them when he first became a cop. He was always the first to ask her to dance. So, she's always called him her toyboy. He never forgets. He's a great man, Tommy is."

Veronica smiled. "He sure is."

"You and him getting it on then? Oops… sorry. Shouldn't have asked that should I?"

She laughed. "Probably not. But in answer to your question. I would like us to." And she began clapping and cheering along with the rest of the crowd gathered around her.

As the music finished, Doyle returned Martha to her chair, where she kissed him on his cheek, told him he was a big flirt, and that she loved him. Then she said, "Now you go dance with that lovely lady of yours," and he was dismissed.

Smiling at him, Veronica said, "Come on, toyboy, I feel like a dance," and taking his hand she headed for the dance floor. Taking her in his arms, Doyle suddenly felt at home.

The rest of the evening went with a swing, as everyone danced and drank the night away. But by one o'clock everyone was safely tucked up in bed.

However, as two o'clock sounded on the church clock, an incident took place outside in the hotel car park. The screeching of car wheels and the shouts of what were believed to be revellers were all the noise that disturbed the night air.

Everyone, including Doyle, slept on.

* * * * *

It was about ten-thirty the following morning before Doyle surfaced. Although he had no hangover, he knew he had certainly enjoyed the celebration of the previous day and night. Climbing out of bed he showered and dressed, then made his way downstairs hoping to find some remnants of breakfast available to him. As entered the dining area, he was lucky. There was at least some bacon and toast still sitting under the heat lamps, plus a fresh pot of coffee.

"Morning, sleepyhead. You've no stamina for a toyboy, have you?"

"Tell me, Veronica, how come you can look as desirable and as gorgeous in a morning after a night of dancing and drinking, as you do in the mortuary?"

"Ouch! Does my Tommy have a hangover then?"

"No, he does not. But he certainly wishes he had gone to bed earlier, taking someone with him instead of dancing all those hours away."

"Tommy Doyle! You are a wicked man!" But despite her supposed indignation she still smiled.

"You won't say that when…"

"Thank God, you're here Tommy. I need you, NOW! Come on." It was Patrick and he didn't look very good. Here was a man who did have a hangover, but that wasn't what was bothering him. "Come on, now man!"

Picking up a slice of toast and a mug of coffee, Doyle followed Patrick. Veronica bringing up the rear, had the impression something was decisively wrong.

Leaving the dining room they headed for the bedrooms, finally coming to a stop outside the bridal suite. Patrick just said, "In there," and he stood aside to let Doyle pass. As Veronica was about to follow, Patrick said, "Family crisis, sorry."

Doyle stopped and turning, said, "It's okay, Patrick, let her through. Remember, she's also a doctor." Patrick hesitated, but then stepped aside to let her pass.

As they entered they found Macy on the bed. She was crying hysterically. So upset was she that no one could understand what she was saying. The medic in Veronica took over and giving instructions she stepped over to the bed.

Taking hold of the young woman, she began talking to her in her calm authoritative but soothing voice. "Okay, Macy. I know something has happened but I need you to calm down and tell me what. Here," and she reached for the glass of water Doyle was passing her, "take a few sips of this. There's a good girl."

"He's… he's… g.g.g.gone!" said Macy, shivering and still sobbing.

"Okay, Macy. Now, tell me, who has gone?"

"Ed… Ed… Edward. He's… He's… gone!"

"What," shouted Patrick. "What the hell do you mean, he's gone? I'll bloody well kill him."

Veronica looked at Doyle, who quickly turned on Patrick, and taking him by the arm he pushed him towards the door, saying, "For God's sake, Pat. Calm down will you? Remember, you're a cop."

"Sorry, sorry, Tommy."

"Okay, Pat. You can stay but you keep that trap shut. Let me and Veronica handle this. As for the rest of you, would you mind leaving the room, please? There are too many people and we need to get to the bottom of this. Okay?" Reluctantly the others left.

Veronica went back to calming Macy down, gently asking her what had happened. Finally, she suggested that the hotel doctor be called and that Macy be given a sedative to calm her completly. This they did, leaving a couple of Macy's Aunties to watch over her. Doyle would talk to her again later, once she was calmer.

Going outside, Doyle, Veronica, and Patrick retired to the bar so they could discuss what had happened. The hotel manager was sent for and access to the outside security camera videos was given. As they watched the screen they were to see, that at approximately two am, Edward had left the hotel and had met up with a couple of men. They appeared to be arguing. Suddenly a fight had ensued, a car pulled up and Edward was bundled into the back. The car had then driven off.

"I think you need to get the tech team to look at the video and see if they can work out the car number plate, and who perhaps those men are?" suggested Doyle.

"I'll ring the Chief now. Ah hell, what has the lad got himself involved in? Be back soon."

Doyle decided to tell Veronica he would not be returning home. "I can arrange a taxi for you. My cost. Sorry about this. Sort of ruins the mini-break doesn't it?"

Veronica looked at him seriously. "If you think I am going to go running home while you stay here to try and solve this mystery, think again, Tommy Doyle. These are your friends, your family, so I'm told, so I'm staying to help. Not sure how much good I will be, but I can help Macy."

Doyle looked at her, thinking 'what a woman.' "What about a change of clothes?"

"I can buy some new ones."

"And work?"

"Stuff that. They can manage without me for once."

"And the new Commissioner? He might sack you!"

"I'm thinking of retiring anyway, so what the hell," and she laughed.

Smiling, he leant over, lightly kissing her on the lips, saying, "Buy what you need, on me. I'll go and extend our stay." Passing her his wallet, he left her to go do some shopping.

Having sorted out their extended stay, Doyle returned to his room and placed a call into Mac. He brought him up to speed, by which time Veronica had returned with several bags, which she dropped onto his bed. Doyle looked on in amazement.

Picking up four of the bags, she passed him his wallet, saying, "It's not that much lighter," then she headed for the door. "Those bags are for you, Tommy. You can't walk around in a dress suit for the next couple of days, can you?" And smiling she closed the door behind her.

Doyle picked up the bags and emptied the contents on the bed. He discovered new underwear, socks, a couple of lightweight shirts, a pair of jeans, and a lightweight jacket – all in his size. 'How, the hell, did she get the size right?' he thought.

Quickly changing into the new gear, Doyle left his room and knocked on Veronica's room door. As she opened the door he leant against the doorframe, saying, "You never cease to amaze me. One question – how the hell did you know my size?"

"It's the M.E. in me. I can assess the size of anybody just by looking at them," and she smiled looking him up and down. "It's easy."

"Come on woman, let's go," he said and turning he started down the corridor, laughing to himself.

* * * * *

Doyle and Veronica headed out to the local police precinct. Doyle wanted to find out if the tech guys had come up with any results from the hotel video. Entering the building he was greeted warmly by a few old faces. As they walked down the corridor, calls of, "Hey, Tommy you old devil, how you doing?" or "Great to see you, Doyle," followed them. There was even the odd wolf whistle from those who appreciated the rear view of Veronica. At the sound, Doyle had smiled, looking sideways at her to watch her reaction. She in turn had put her hand behind her back, giving them the middle finger. Very unladylike but what the hell, it was her way of coping with men's reactions to her. Unfortunately, this only created more whistles and comments such as, "Way to go, Doyle!" Veronica and Doyle just laughed, both were used to the repartee of a police precinct. After all, what the officers did for a job was often dangerous, so this was their way of unwinding; releasing some of the stress and tension they suffered.

Walking into the tech office, they found Patrick waiting for them. He was inspecting some print-outs, which he handed to Doyle. "The guys are checking the mug shots to see if they can find a name, and they're running a check on the car plate. Only got a partial so it might take time."

"Thanks, Pat. How's Macy this morning?"

"She's still upset. The local doctor has her under sedation. What the hell is Edward playing at? What's he got himself wrapped up in? I swear if my little girl gets hurt I'll kill him!"

"Calm down, Pat. Whatever it is we'll sort it. I'm not going home until we do, okay?"

Patrick looked at Doyle. "You're a good mate, Tommy. Wish you'd never left the force."

Doyle only smiled in response, shrugging his shoulders as if to say, 'ces't la vie.'

Looking at the photos of the guys, Doyle's nose began to twitch. Something started to stir in his memory. It felt as if he knew one of them. The question was, where from and who was he? 'Hell,' he thought. 'Who is he?' He hated it when he couldn't recall a face easily. Maybe it was time he retired?

"The best we can do is to say it could be a Dodge. Mmm... maybe a Dynasty," said the technician who had been searching for a match for the car in the video. "If it is, then it should be easy to find as there weren't that many made. Though, with only a partial number plate it's still gonna be difficult to pinpoint it down. And it's possible, the plate could have been changed, especially if it's from out of state!"

Doyle felt his nose twitch again. Something about the car and the guy was beginning to bother him. They had to be linked. If only he could work out what it was.

"Okay, guys, good work. Keep checking and let me know what you find," said Patrick. "Come on, Tommy, Veronica, let's go for a coffee. I've one hell of a hangover."

Laughing, Doyle and Veronica followed Patrick out of the room, and down the corridor to the canteen. As they sat and had a well-needed drink, Doyle asked, "Macy has no idea what Edward might be caught up in?"

"Nah... she said he never said anything to her. Although... she did say he had been worried over the last few days, but she had put that down to wedding nerves. I just don't get it, Tommy, the boy seemed so straight-laced. His mother and father are churchgoers. Uncle is a priest upstate. He's got a good job – sells real estate. Works for the family firm. No convictions. Squeaky clean. Hell, any man would want him for a son-in-law. Honest, hardworking, and straight. At least I thought so up until now." Patrick was clearly frustrated, as well as being upset by the way he felt his new son-in-law had let his daughter and him down.

"Pat, don't jump to conclusions. We don't know what has happened, and until we do, you shouldn't be ready to convict the lad. For all we know, he might be in trouble not of his making, thus putting him in danger. We need to find out quickly if that is so."

Patrick gave Doyle a funny grin, knowing his pal was right. Then tapping Doyle's hand he said, "You're right. Thanks, Tommy. And thanks for being here. And for staying. And you too, Veronica, for looking after my baby last night. Much appreciated."

Veronica smiled. "I am sure that whatever trouble Edward is in, Tommy here, will help you get it sorted. I've seen this man in action lots of times and I know he'll do his best for you. And I was happy to help with Macy. She's a lovely girl."

Doyle was pleasantly surprised at Veronica's praises of him. Little did she know that she had actually boosted his morale. He was also grateful for her handling of his god-daughter.

"Pat, I think I'd like to go see where Edward works. Maybe check out what he does, talk to any staff, see if they know anything. Also might be an idea to check his phone calls at home. We need to treat this like any other abduction case. Make it official. Check out the family, on both sides."

"What. Doyle are you crazy or what?" said Patrick shocked.

Doyle held his hand up to stop his friend from speaking. "Have you thought this could be payback for you doing something to some perp? We need to keep a close watch on Macy. Time to do it by the book. You can't sweep it under the rug. Get the press involved. The longer this goes on, the longer we risk losing him."

"Wow, Tommy, you mean business don't you?" Patrick sat shaking his head. "Hell, I know you're right. I don't like it but you're right. Let's go talk to the Chief?" Doyle agreed and leaving Veronica in the canteen the two of them went upstairs to talk to the Chief of Police, who just happened to be Patrick's cousin.

After they had gone, Veronica was not left alone for long, being joined pretty much soon enough by several officers who had called into the canteen for their coffee fix. Now she knew what it felt like to be treated like a celebratory. The older men were mainly interested in her relationship with Doyle. Many of them having known his ex-wife. The younger ones were hoping the relationship was purely professional. She let them all down gently. Neither confirming nor denying anything. Just as she was wondering how to escape the interrogation Doyle came to her rescue.

"Okay, guys, enough. You have pestered my lady enough. Come on, sweetheart, let me rescue you from these lecherous beasts," and he laughed as he took her hand and led her towards the door. As they left Veronica turned and blew a kiss across the room to them. The whistles and cheers could be heard all the way down the corridor.

Doyle was laughing as he walked. "My God, woman. I can't leave you alone for ten minutes can I before you have them eating out of your hand." Taking her hand in his he headed for the car park where a blues and twos were waiting for them.

"Where are we going?" she asked.

"To visit a realtor. Edwards' company. Going to talk to his Dad and the staff. Patrick's ringing ahead so they know we're coming. I was going to leave you there but thought better of it. Your dangerous, Doc," and he laughed again as they both climbed into the car.

Fifteen minutes later the police car pulled up outside the office of Carlton & Flagg Realtor. It was quite an impressive building with a few decent cars parked out front. Entering the office, Martin Cresswell was waiting to greet them. "It's great to see you again, Tommy. Sorry, I missed the wedding, only flew in late last night." Spotting Veronica he extended his hand to her, "Hello, Matthew Carlton, Edward's father, pleased to meet you."

"This is Veronica Martin, my friend from home who attended the wedding with me. Can we talk somewhere privately, Matthew?"

"Sure, follow me. Hold my calls please, Cissy," Mathew said as led the way to the rear of the building and his private office. "Please, take a seat. Can I get you anything?"

Sitting, both and Doyle and Veronica declined the offer of refreshments. Then Doyle got stuck in straight away. "You been away, Matthew?"

"Yes, I have been negotiating a big land deal down in Mexico. It's been a nightmare I can tell you. Lots of problems but hopefully they will get sorted. So, what's all this nonsense about Edward. What's he done wrong. Not a traffic violation? Got drunk or something? You know boys will be boys on their stag night," and he laughed.

To Doyle, the sound seemed forced, as if the man was under pressure. "Tell me, Matthew have you been having any business problems recently? Anyone causing a nuisance? Being difficult? Threatening you, maybe?"

"What... NO... No, no. Everything is fine. Hunky-dory in fact. We've been under pressure a little since buying Joe, my ex-partner out, but that's all passed now. Why do you ask?"

"I am wondering if the guys who have kidnapped Edward..."

"What! Kidnapped! Who said Edward was kidnapped?" shouted Matthew.

"Well, it appears that, the manner in which he was taken last night, leads police to believe that he was, in fact, kidnapped! I thought Patrick had told you that?"

"Well, yes, but he… he… he said he was missing. Not kidnapped."

Doyle shook his head. Trust Patrick to leave it to him to drop the bad news. "The thing is Matthew, last night at two am, while his new wife and all their wedding guests were sleeping, Edward slipped out of the hotel, met up with two guys of an unsavoury nature, had an argument, and was bundled into a black car and driven away. As of yet, the police have no understanding as to why that would happen. Hence why I am involved and am here asking you the question. Is something going on that we should know about? If so, what is it? If we don't know, we can't help you, or Edward. And it could cost him his life. So, I ask you again is there anything wrong?"

Matthew didn't reply immediately. Instead, he took a deep breath to calm himself. Finally, he said, "No. There is nothing wrong. I am sure that whatever Edward is up to, it's just a stupid boy prank. Now if that is all, I have work to do."

Having in effect been dismissed, Doyle was left with little choice but to leave. Rising he said, "As you've been away I don't suppose you'll mind my having a quick word with the staff. Just to check that no one has been in the office threatening Edward?"

"If you must. Thank you for calling. Goodbye."

As they left Matthews office, Doyle's nose began to twitch again. He would have a lot to say to Patrick but first, he'd chat with the staff. Starting with Cissy, the boss's secretary.

Approaching her, he smiled warmly, "Hi, Cissy, I'm Tommy, I don't if you've heard but Edward has gone missing and I'm helping the police find him. I wondered if you would answer a couple of questions, please."

"If it's okay with Mr. Carlton, then yes. What would you like to know?" she replied.

"Has there been anyone in the office recently, while Mr. Carlton, Senior was away, who perhaps behaved in a threatening manner? Caused a problem for Mr. Edward?"

"No. Not that I'm aware of. But I am not Mr. Edwards's secretary so I wouldn't know. And besides, I've been away for the last week. With Mr. Carlton not working, he said I could take a holiday," and she smiled sweetly. Doyle looked at her and thought, 'I bet he did. A holiday. Probably in the same place as Mr. Carlton, if I'm not wrong." Smiling he thanked her.

As he was about to leave he stopped and asked, "Where is the rest of the staff? Are they on lunch?"

Cissy swallowed, before replying, "Mr. Carlton has given them the day off. An extended weekend in celebration of Mr. Edwards' wedding." Doyle just nodded and left the building.

Climbing into the back of the waiting police car, Doyle instructed the driver to drop them off at the hotel. He wanted to make a couple of phone calls; one to his pal Mac, whom he needed to research some information for him.

As they drove along, Veronica said, "He seemed very matter of fact about his son going missing on his wedding night, didn't he? Do you think he's telling the truth?"

Doyle took her hand and kissed it absent-mindedly, before saying, "No, Veronica. I think he's lying through his high teeth. The question is – why?" Nothing more was said, but he didn't let go of her hand until they reached the hotel.

* * * * *

The phone rang on Mac's desk. Slowly picking it up, he said, "Mackintosh."

"Hi, Mac, it's Tommy. Are you free to chat?"

"Tommy, my lad, how are things going? You still helping up there with the missing groom?"

"Yea. Gonna take a couple of days. I wondered if you could do some research for me, please? I don't want to ask here as there are local connections. I'm trying to do this under the radar, so to speak."

Surprised, Mac said, "Sure, Tommy, ask away. It May take me 'til tomorrow as I have the new Commissioner breathing down my neck, so I may have to wait until he's gone home. What is it you want to know? Fire away?"

Doyle explained what he wanted Mac to research for him, starting with the history of Carlton & Flagg realtors. He wanted all he could get on both guys. He also asked Mac to check their records for the number plate and car plus, having asked Patrick to send the photos of the two perps, he wanted Mac to get someone to go through their mug shots. Finally, he wanted Mac to go through Doyle's own files and look for some cases to do with embezzlement, dating back five years ago. Mac had access to Doyle's brownstone, knowing the alarm access and filing cabinet codes. He was the only person Doyle had ever trusted them with.

"Okay, Tommy. Will do. As I said, will access the records later today when the Commissioner has gone home."

"That bad is it?"

"Bad! I've just about got my resignation written. Not sure I can stand much more of the man. He's spent the last two weeks in and out of my office…," Mac's voice suddenly dropped to a whisper, "…talk of the devil…," then he spoke louder, "great, got to go, thanks for the information. Will get back to you if I need anything else, Office Myers," and the phone went dead.

To Doyle, it sounded as if Mac was having a rough time. With nothing else to do until Mac came back to him, Doyle decided he would take Veronica to visit Granny Martha. She was usually a font of all information, maybe she could shed some light on things. Even if she didn't know anything, he couldn't be in the area without spending some 'family time' with her. Heavens knew how long she had; although knowing her, she would try to outlive them all. His other reason for seeing her was to get her views on Veronica. He wanted to know whether she approved of her or not.

Knocking on Veronica's door he found her looking upset. "What's the matter? Tell me?"

"I've just had a call from the office. The new Commissioner has been in. He's threatening to sack all the staff. I'm bloody angry!"

"What! The bastard. Hell, Veronica, I am so sorry. This is my fault. I brought you here."

"No, Tommy, no. I chose to stay. And besides I had days of due to me. I'm sorry if I worried you, but I think I'd better get back. The staff isn't capable of standing up to that man, but I damn well am. No-one, and I don't care who the hell he is, can come in and threaten my staff while I'm in charge. No one!"

Taking her in his arms, he told her, "I'll drive you back. Come on, gather your stuff together. I need to call at the office anyway to grab some files." As she started to argue, he stopped her saying, "Don't argue woman or else. It's not a long drive. I'll be there and back before dinner. Come on. Let's go."

Smiling at the way he had taken control, she did as he said, and grabbing her stuff she followed him out of the hotel to the car.

An hour and a half later Doyle dropped Veronica off at home, pecked her on the cheek, told her he would ring later, and then quickly left. He needed to get to the brownstone, so he could let Mac know not to bother calling. He hoped Veronica would be able to sort the matter at the mortuary out with little problem. This new Commissioner was certainly stirring things up. If he carried on like this he could see the district losing some of its best officers, as well as other personnel. He wondered if the Governor was aware of all the shenanigans going on? Probably not.

Doyle had only just arrived at the brownstone when Mac turned up. Surprised, he asked Doyle what he was doing there? Having explained about Veronica and why they had returned, Mac said, "That man had better be ready for fireworks because when they go up all hell is going to break loose. I don't know who I'll pity more – him or the Governor, ha-ha!"

Doyle laughed. "I agree, Mac. Any joy on the information I asked for?"

Picking up his carry case, Mac opened it and passed a bundle of papers across to Doyle. "I hope these help. If you need anything else, let me know. For now, I'm off to O' Malley's for a bite to eat and a drink. I need both. You coming?"

"You go on ahead. Get em' set up. I'll join you in about ten minutes. Just want to grab a bag to put this lot in. Then I'm driving back up to the hotel. Might as well read this lot in my room later."

"Did you not get much sleep last night then, Tommy?" and Mac winked.

Picking up a screwed piece of paper from off the desk, Tommy aimed it at Mac, and laughing said, "You have a dirty mind, Pete Mackintosh. Go order the food and drinks." Laughing Mac left the office.

After he had gone, Doyle thought about the last couple of days and wondered if he had missed his opportunity. Veronica was certainly a woman worth having. The question was – was he worth having in return? 'Hell, Doyle,' he told himself. 'Get your mind on the job, now!' and picking out and packing the papers he wanted, along with those that mac had brought him, Doyle locked up the brownstone and headed for O' Malley's Bar.

Nothing more was said about Veronica, other than to discuss the threatened staff sackings and how angry she had been hearing about it. After they had eaten, Doyle left for the hotel upstate, while Mac returned to the office. He had thought of something that he wanted to do. It was called covering your back. If he was going to retire, then he needed to ensure that Doyle, as well as himself were secure. You just didn't know what this new Commissioner was capable of? It seemed he was on a crusade of some sort. The more he thought about it, the more retirement appealed to him.

* * * * *

Doyle got back to the hotel fairly late so didn't get a chance to read through all the paperwork provided by Mac. The next morning, he checked in with Patrick, only to discover there was no further news. No messages, no ransom. It appeared as though Edward had just disappeared from the face of the earth. Macy was inconsolable. Not yet ready to face her, Doyle decided to make the promised visit to see Granny Martha. She in turn was delighted to see him.

"Come in, Thomas, come in. It's so good to see you," she said as if she hadn't already seen him at the wedding. Doyle wondered if perhaps she was starting to lose her memory. He hoped not.

"And how is my beautiful girl, then," he said, kissing her on her weathered cheek and giving her a gentle squeeze with his arms.

"All the better for seeing you. Come, tell me what you've been up to since I last saw you. And tell me more about Veronica. I want to know it all."

Laughing, Doyle followed her through into her sitting room. Looking around, memories started flooding back. All the happy times he had spent sitting in this room, listening to music, watching Martha knitting or sewing, and her talking to him. She had been there when he had first become a cop - when he had first been promoted - the first time he had brought Mary home. He stopped, this was one of the few times he had thought about his ex-wife. Mary had been lovely. He had loved her. But, she couldn't take the life of being a cop's wife and so she had left, eventually marrying a grocer.

"What you are thinking, Thomas?" asked Martha.

Doyle looked up and smiled. "I was thinking of all the happy moments I've had in this room. You were good to me, Martha. Very good. Took the place of my mother. I never realised how much I missed her after she died, until I stayed here. Dad was always working. And then suddenly, he was gone."

"They would both have been proud of you, Thomas. You've always been a good man. It was a pity about Mary, but… these things happen. Casualty of war, as they say. Still, you got a new lady now. She seems a very nice girl."

Doyle laughed, "I'll tell her you approve. Girl, indeed. She's all woman, Martha. All woman." And they both laughed.

"Can I ask you something?" said Doyle.

"Of course, son. What do you want to know?"

"Do you know anything about Edward? What he's got himself involved in maybe?"

Martha sat thinking for a while. "To be honest, Thomas, I'm worried about the lad. But, it's not Edward who's the problem. I always say, you should always look to the father. The son can only go wrong if the father is bad. Yours was a good strong man, and so are you. Look to the father, Thomas. Look to the father."

Doyle realised that would probably be all he would get from Martha, and yet strangely, it matched his own feelings. He'd had a sense the father was holding something back. There was something wrong with that man and he was determined to get to the bottom of it. If only to protect his god-daughter, Macy. Smiling at Martha, the rest of the evening was spent reminiscing. Looking at old photographs, something they usually did when he visited. Something he felt he hadn't been doing too often in recent years. 'Time to make amends,' he thought.

Returning to the hotel, after his visit to Martha, Doyle ordered room service and settled down to finish reading the paperwork. This time making notes about various people and elements that appeared similar to Edwards' disappearance. Roundabout midnight, he fell asleep still reading his old files.

* * * * *

When Doyle woke the following morning he was surprised to find himself still dressed in the clothes he had worn the day before. Feeling stiff, he gathered the paperwork together, dropping them into his carry case. Then he took a hot shower to refresh himself, and dressed in some of the clothes Veronica had bought for him. As he looked in the mirror to comb his hair, he realised what taste the lady had.

"Well," he said out loud, "If you're the cat Veronica and I'm the mouse, bring it on girl. I'm yours to catch," and he laughed at himself.

Leaving the hotel Doyle climbed into his car, heading for the precinct, having arranged to meet up with Patrick. The information Mac had managed to dig up might come as a surprise to Pat. Only time would tell.

Arriving at the police station, Doyle asked to see Patrick. As he waited he looked at the wanted posters. Seeing someone he recognised he pulled the photo off the wall. About to say something to the desk Sergeant, a voice said, "You causing vandalism in a police station, Tommy?" It was Patrick.

Laughing, Doyle passed him the photofit picture, and said, "You can scrub him from your records. He's dead."

"What! How do you know?"

"He drowned, about eighteen months ago. He was one of JoJo Grimondi's boys. Got caught up in some gang warfare type of incident. Ended up in the Diamond Valley Lake Reservoir, with a pair of concrete boots. Mac can send you all the details. Not sure why you didn't get the update, but I know this for a fact as I worked on the case with Mac."

Patrick looked at Tommy, with almost a new respect. "You working with the force?"

Doyle nodded. "Occasionally I do the odd under-cover work. I can usually get to go places some of the cops can't. Plus I have a good underground network. Mac and I have helped each other out ever since I left the force. Works well."

Tapping the photo, Patrick said, "Thanks for this, Tommy. It will go towards closing another case. Now, what else can I do for you?"

Smiling, Doyle said, "Let's go somewhere private. I err... have some information that might interest you."

A look of both surprise, then concern crossed Patrick's face, but seeing Doyle's smile and having just been handed a closed case with no effort on his part, he just said, "Follow me, mastermind!"

Entering an office on the first floor, Patrick closed the door, indicating Doyle should take a seat. Once settled Doyle began to lay out the papers he had brought with him. Starting with the history of one - Christopher Walter Fisher.

"Who the bloody hell is Fisher?" asked Patrick.

Doyle took his time in answering. "Christopher Walter Fisher is in fact... Mr. Matthew Carlton, realtor, and member of the parish church, father of Edward. He is also a wanted man."

"What!" Patrick almost shouted. "You gotta be kidding me?"

Doyle sat shaking his head. "Afraid not, Pat."

Patrick was left stunned. He suddenly felt sick to the pit of his stomach. About to speak, Doyle interrupted him, "No threats of killing him. The best way is to string him up for the crimes he's committed. Besides we still need to get Edward back."

"What, I don't want that little worm being married to my baby. She'll have to divorce him."

"Pat. That isn't up to you. If Edward is innocent in all this, AND I think he is, then that's down to Macy to make the decision. It's nothing to do with you. All we, all you have to do, is stand by her decision. Remember that, okay?"

Reluctantly, Patrick nodded his head. He knew Doyle was right. It was Macy's decision. He would stand by her, whatever she decided. Finally, he said, "You're right, Tommy. Always did have your head on right. Whoever screwed you over, making you leave the job didn't do the force any favours. Thanks. You have our Macy's well-being at heart. Thanks, man," and he leant forward to shake Doyle's hand. "Okay, tell me what do we do now?"

Knowing Pat had got his act together, settled Doyle's mind. "Well, Pat, this is what I suggest..."

and he set out his ideas of how they should approach the situation of the missing Edward, starting with his father.

* * * * *

Three hours later, two unmarked cars rolled into the car park of Carlton & Flagg Realtors. Stepping out of the cars were, Doyle, Patrick with both search and arrest warrants in his pocket, and four other plainclothes officers. Entering the realtors' office, Doyle turned the door sign to closed as the other officers told the waiting customers to quietly leave the premises, which they did. While this had been happening, Cissy the secretary had slipped into Carlton's office to inform of their presence.

"What the hell do you think you're doing. Get out of here!" The man stood with his hand in the air pointing towards the door, as if expecting the men to obey without question.

It was at this point that Patrick, stepping forward, slammed both warrants into Carlton's hand, saying, "Matthew Carlton, a.k.a. Christopher Walter Fisher, you are under arrest for embezzlement, suspected connections to criminal enterprises, and suspected involvement with a number of murders. You have the right to remain silent. Anything you say can, and will, be used against you in a court of law. You have the right to an attorney. If you cannot afford an attorney, one will be appointed for you."

One of the officers stepped forward and taking hold of Carlton's hands he secured them behind the man's back with handcuffs. Patrick then continued speaking, "I am also serving you with a warrant to search these premises. I am also notifying you that we have the authority to remove all documents and computers that we feel are relevant or necessary to further our investigation. Take him away."

"Stop. You can't do this. They'll kill Edward. Please. My son's life is in danger."

"You should have thought of that before breaking the law, or allowing him to marry my daughter. Get him out of here. I'll see you back at the station."

"No, don't, please, please..." But his pleas went unheard.

After he had gone, the forensic team moved in fast. The other offices moved all the staff into a separate room, each being interviewed separately in the visitors' room. After their details were taken and confirmed, the staff were allowed to go home, with a warning not to leave the district. Cissy, Carlton's secretary, was the last to be seen. This was done by Patrick, with Doyle in attendance, before they returned to the precinct to question Carlton/Fisher himself. Whilst it turned out Doyle's intuition about there being something romantic going on between the two was correct, she was, however, not involved in anything else untoward. Nor did she know anything about any criminal activities. She left the building exceedingly upset that she had been taken in by her boss.

* * * * *

Entering the interview room, Carlton's lawyer was ready for action. Unfortunately for him, Patrick struck first. "Now, Mr. Carlton, or should I say, Christopher Walter Fisher, what do you have to tell me regarding the whereabouts of Edward Carlton?"

"My client has nothing to say, other than his son Edward is in danger and unless you release him immediately he will be killed."

Looking at the lawyer, Patrick said, "Well unfortunately for your client, I am not at liberty to do that. You see, Mr. Fisher here is wanted by at least two other state forces on very serious charges. They are, at this very moment, in discussion with my superiors as to who actually has jurisdiction. They have already dispatched officers to come and interview your client about those charges. However, my concern at this moment is for the safe return of Edward Carlton. So, I suggest you start talking… fast."

Looking first at his lawyer who nodded, Carlton/Fisher leant forward, saying, "You don't understand, these guys are mean, real mean. If I talk, they'll kill Edward. I don't know where he is. And they haven't been in touch with me." He sounded quite distressed.

Patrick looked at Doyle, not sure where to go next. Doyle nodded his head as if asking for Pat's permission to ask a question. Pat nodded back. "Tell me, Fisher, what exactly do these guys want from you," asked Doyle.

Carlton again looked at his lawyer, who nodded, before answering, "I have the deeds to a certain piece of land. I acquired it some years ago from an old woman. She lived on her own and I befriended her. I err… talked her into signing it over to me. The great grandson wants it back."

Scowling, a sudden thought hit Doyle. "Where is this land?"

Hesitating before answering, Fisher replied, "East of Marshall County Canyon Park. Can't remember the old woman's name. Was a foreign name. She said she had no relatives."

"So you took advantage of her age and loneliness, then robbed her of her only asset; you scumbag," snarled Patrick.

"Inspector, I'll thank you to not call my client such names," the lawyer snapped back.

As Patrick was about to answer, Doyle butted in. "Well, well, well, you have got yourself in a mess, haven't you, Mr. Fisher. What a quandary. Do you know, if it wasn't for the fact that I believe Edward knows nothing about your underhand dealings or your past, I would leave him to be fed to the fishes? Come on Patrick, we need to make a phone call, urgently," and standing up Doyle left the room. Patrick suspending the interview followed shortly afterwards.

"What the hell was all that about, Tommy? Do you know something?"

Doyle looked Patrick in the eyes. "I'm getting old, Pat. I've had a niggle going around in my mind ever since I looked at the photos of the two guys who kidnapped Edward. Fisher has just confirmed that niggle. Damn, I should have got it earlier. Come on, we need to speak to Mac, NOW," and he set off down the corridor.

* * * * *

Hanging up the phone fifteen minutes later, Doyle cursed himself. Why the hell hadn't he recognised the perp earlier. Shaking his head in disgust, he thought, 'Perhaps it's time I did retire from this job?'

Patrick, having been updating his Chief, returned to the office. "You ready for round two, Tommy?"

Nodding, Doyle said, "Lead the way, Pat."

The interview with Matthew Carlton, a.k.a. Christopher Walter Fisher, continued into the early afternoon. There wasn't much else they could do after that, other than wait for news from Mac, who had instigated a search for Edward closer to him. Doyle was still annoyed by his lack of ability to have recognised the man in the photo. It had been one of JoJo Grimondi's heavies. One Doyle had met on more than occasion. The waiting was frustrating for him.

Two hours later the news came in. Edward had been found – hurt – but alive!

"Thank God," announced Pat. For once, Doyle agreed with him.

Patrick decided he would put Fisher out of his misery, by telling him his son had been found. The man burst into tears. As did his wife when she discovered the truth of all that had been going on. During the day she had been in church praying for the safe return of her son. Before leaving she had looked at her husband, a man she never really knew, saying, "I gave you the best years of my life. You are not the man I thought you were when I married you. You have cheated on me, numerous times, but still I forgave you. You have put our son in danger and done nothing to save him. For that, I will never forgive you. BUT, I will ask God to. As far as I am concerned, I never want to look on your face again. Goodbye Matthew, or whatever your real name is," and on that comment, she turned and left the police station.

Macy, Edward's new bride, travelled with Patrick, to the County Community Hospital at Norwalk, where Edward had been taken. Doyle would settle up at the hotel and follow in his own car.

* * * * *

Two hours later Doyle arrived at the hospital. Finding Edward's room he knocked on the door and opened it. "Can I come in?"

Macy stood up, and going to him she threw her arms around him, hugging him tightly. "Thank you, Uncle Tommy. You saved my Edward."

Feeling slightly embarrassed, Doyle laughingly said, "Hey, it wasn't all down to me, sweetheart. There was your Dad, and the guys at the precinct working on this as well, you know!"

Letting him go, Macy looked up at Tommy, "Yea, I know, but you knew who the bad guys were. Who had taken Edward, and you made sure he was rescued," and she hugged him once again.

Doyle knew he was beat, so he accepted the hugs willingly. It had been a long time since she'd been a little girl and had hugged him so strongly. Finally, she let him go. Doyle, looked at Edward, "You okay, Ed?"

"Not bad, Mr. Doyle. Thanks for getting me out."

Doyle waved his hand as if to say it was nothing. Pat said, "How about we go get a coffee? Leave these two lovebirds to talk." Agreeing, Doyle and Pat left the room.

As they walked down the corridor, they bumped into Veronica coming the other way. "Hey, Veronica. How are you doing? Have you heard the news? They've found Edward."

Veronica, dressed in hospital whites, made Doyle scowl in wonder. "You working, Doc?" he asked.

Smiling at him, she said, "Covering for a friend who's been taken ill. Got wounded by a drug addict in the mortuary of all places. They thought there might be drugs in the body so they needed me to do the autopsy, just in case. Was clear. Great news about Edward though. Well done guys."

"We're off for a coffee, fancy joining us?" asked Pat. "I wanted to thank you."

"What for. He's no doubt the one who solved the case," she laughed, pointing at Doyle.

"He did, but no, I wanted to thank you for looking after my Macy, the day Edward went missing. And for checking up on her afterwards. I know you went to visit her a couple of times. So, thanks, Veronica."

Smiling, she patted Pat's arm, saying, "You're very welcome, Pat. How is she doing now?"

"Over the moon, Edward is safe. We've left them alone. That's why we're off for a coffee. Gonna join us? My treat."

Agreeing to join them in the hospital coffee shop once she'd changed, Veronica disappeared, while Doyle and Pat carried on to order the drinks. Just as they were about to enter the coffee shop they bumped into Mac.

"Tommy, just the man I wanted to see."

Doyle introduced Mac to Patrick, inviting him to join them for a drink. With Veronica arriving shortly afterward the four of them settled at a table in the corner of the room. Doyle was eager to get the news on JoJo Grimondi's arrest, as that is what he had organised with Mac when he had rung him.

"Boy, did you give me a doozy there, Tommy! Best collar I've had for months. Couldn't believe it when we burst in and found Edward in Grimondi's warehouse. And what made it even better, was that Grimondi himself was there, along with the two guys in your photo. Talk about getting the jackpot. Thanks, pal."

Doyle laughed. "You're welcome, but Pat had a lot to do with it as well."

"Hey, Tommy, don't sell yourself short; couldn't have done it without you. Oh! And Veronica, of course," said Pat.

The look of surprise on her face caused the other three to laugh. "All in a mortuary doc days' work, Sir," she replied, raising her coffee in salute.

Whilst they drank their coffee they chatted about the part Mac had played in solving the finding of Edward. He'd managed to trace JoJo to his warehouse, really a derelict building out in the sticks. "Mind you, it's a very secure derelict building," Mac told them.

Surrounding the place they had gate-crashed the party, catching JoJo red-handed. Edward had later told them about the deeds for the land. He had been told a few days before the wedding that his father had been kidnapped and he had to get the deeds to the two guys in the video. When Edward couldn't contact his father, he went about trying to find the papers. However, no matter where he searched, he couldn't find them.

On the night of his wedding, he left the hotel, explained to the guys he couldn't find the papers. An argument had ensued, and before he knew it he was being bundled into the back of a car. What followed wasn't a pleasant experience. The guys had tried to beat the location of the papers out of him. And even though he kept telling them he didn't know where they were, they still didn't believe him. Two days later they said they had contacted his father and he had better come up with the goods, or else Edward could kiss his life goodbye. Edward had honestly thought he was going to die, so was very relieved when Mac and the police burst in and arrested his captors.

Looking at Doyle, Mac asked, "Do you know what papers he was referring to, Tommy?"

"Yea. The land is east of Marshall County Canyon Park. It belonged to the old Don's Grandmother. The old Don never bothered about it, thinking she had sold it, as that is what he was told. JoJo must have researched the land files and decided he wanted it back. Carlton/Fisher had conned the old dear out of it. Therefore, in JoJo's eyes, he'd conned him. Payback time as far as JoJo was concerned."

"Well, I have to say, I'm happy," laughed Mac.

"In that case, dinner is on you tonight," laughed Doyle in return.

"Deal. You joining us, Pat, Veronica?"

While Veronica was up for dinner, Pat declined, saying he was taking his daughter, Macy, out for a quiet father/daughter dinner. "Thanks, but maybe next time."

"Deal," said Mac, and the three of them went their separate ways.

* * * * *

Back at the brownstone later, Doyle was finishing getting ready. He had chosen to wear the last of the shirts Veronica had chosen for him. He liked her style, and as she was joining them for dinner, he wanted to make an effort.

Arriving at O' Malley's Bar & Grill, Tommy was pleased to see Mac and Veronica waiting for him. They were sat at a table in the corner, deep in conversation. It allowed him a few moments to observe them both. This last job had got him seriously considering retirement and he was wondering how he was going to tell his two closest friends of his proposed decision.

Veronica must have sensed his presence as she looked up and stared straight at him. She liked what she saw. He smiled at her. She smiled back and then waved. Walking over to join them, Mac met him part way. "Drink, Tommy?"

"Beer, please, Mac. Have you ordered?"

"Not yet. Thought you might like a steak tonight, seeing as how it's a celebration!"

Laughing, Doyle went to join Veronica. He kissed her on the cheek before sitting down. Looking her over, he whistled low, then said, "Very nice, Doc. You scrub up well, every time I see you."

Veronica pretended indignation, saying, "You certainly know how to flatter a girl, Tommy Doyle," then she laughed.

Doyle smiled, leant over and whispered, "You look beautiful."

"Now, that's what I call a compliment, Tommy."

"Okay you two stop the smooching and let's order." Doyle and Veronica looked at Mac as if he had insulted them, then they both cracked up laughing.

Finally, Veronica said, "I will have you know, Inspector Mackintosh, that I've long since passed the smooching stage. I'm into something more exciting, now," and she winked at him, causing Mac to laugh and say, "Ooohh... you sexy girl... you!!"

The evening improved from there; with laughter and teasing on all sides. As the night started to draw to a close, Mac suddenly got serious. He was about to drop a bombshell on Tommy and was a little reluctant to start. Plucking up the courage he began.

"Tommy, I need to tell you something."

Doyle looked at Mac, a questioning look on his face. "What?" he asked.

Taking a breath, Mac said, "I'm finishing."

Doyle was stunned, not sure what Mac meant. About to say finishing what, it dawned him what Mac meant. "When?"

"In a month. On my official retirement date, the twenty-fifth of next month. I'm taking my pension, and I'm off."

Now Doyle was genuinely stunned. To be honest he had expected Mac to be taken out of the precinct in a coffin – so to speak. He didn't seem like the retiring kind. The job was his life."

The silence stretched between them, until finally Mac said, "Well, are you gonna say something or what?"

"This is a sudden decision. Why are you doing it now? I thought you were gonna wait another year?"

Swallowing, then sighing, Mac told them, "I can't take any more of the politics. And the new

Commissioner, well, he's driving me and the guys crazy. I just can't stand him. I very nearly smacked him yesterday. In front of the Governor."

"Hell, Mac, what happened?"

"Well, we'd picked JoJo up, great score for the precinct. The Governor had heard so he popped in to say congrats and as he was talking to me, in comes the Commissioner and starts accepting all the praise. Now, if it had just been me, I wouldn't bothered. But, that s-o-b was stealing the limelight from the reast of the guys. They don't get enough praise, this collar was as much theirs as mine to have. That man pissed me off. He stood there and bared faced lied that it was all down to him; his reorganisation of the precinct had got the job done. He wanted all the bloody praise for himself. I'd had it. Couldn't take it anymore."

"Wow, Mac, you should have smacked him. I sure as hell would have." The comment caused all three of them to laugh, knowing Doyle may well have carried out his threat had he been there. "Did you say anything?"

"Couldn't really. But, it made me realise that I can't go on working for an asshole. Just before the Governor left, I handed him an envelope. Notice of my intention not to extend my stay, but to take my pension in full when I retire next month. It's done and dusted."

Doyle wasn't sure what to say. He wanted to both congratulate and commiserate with his friend, but wasn't sure which to do first. "If that's your decision, I'm with you all the way, Mac. Always have been, always will be," and Doyle stretched his hand across the table to shake Mac's.

Coughing, Veronica brought attention to herself. Looking at both guys, she finally said, "Well, if we're confessing stuff, I might as well cough up some news too. Err… I'm leaving the precinct as well."

"What," said Mac and Doyle in unison. "When? Why?"

"Same reason. Can't stand the Commissioner. When I learnt he was threatening to sack my staff I went back early from the hotel Tommy and I were staying at."

"Ah! Sorry, Doc, I forgot to ask what happened, didn't I?" said Doyle feeling annoyed.

"Not your fault, Tommy, You've been very busy. So, don't worry. Anyway, when I got back he had indeed threatened most of my staff. When I asked him what he was playing at, he told me, 'I don't play games. I run a tight ship and I think changes are going to be made in this department. You are too lackadaisical in the way you run this place. Taking time off whenever you feel like it. That does not set an example as a leader.'"

"Bloody hell, I'll go in there and smack him for you," said Doyle.

Laughing, Veronica told him, "As much as you are my hero, Tommy Doyle, I don't think that would be a good idea. Besides, I am a big girl and I can take care of myself, trust me," and she smiled to take any sting out of the comment. "Anyway. I looked him in the eye, and I said, 'For your information, Commissioner, my ship runs perfectly well. I trust my staff, even if I am not in the office. And they all know exactly where to contact me, if necessary. I am on call twenty four hours a day, seven days a week, which is probably more than you are. As for the time I've just taken off, as of last week, I am still owed exactly ten months' worth of holidays, for which I have not yet been paid. So, as regards sacking my staff, if you do, then you can sack me. However, I warn you, that you had better start finding the money you owe me, because I will be coming for it.' And then I walked out of his office before he could say anything. I went to see the union guy. When I returned, I didn't give the s-o-b a chance to fire me, I quit. What he doesn't know is, I've been offered a job at the Hospital morgue. But, I'm still thinking about it."

"Wow," said Doyle and Mac. "Now that's the way to do it!"

"Phew," went Doyle. Then, taking a breath, he said, "Okay, you guys It seems as if this is quite an evening of announcements. So, I might as well tell you, this last case has really got to me. The fact I couldn't recognise JoJo's heavy from the photo, or remember him, has really screwed my mind up. I've been thinking that perhaps, maybe it's time I retired. As such, I'm thinking of selling the brownstone and moving up to the house in Twin Peaks."

"What!" said Veronica, sounding a little upset by his announcement. "You're going to leave?"

"Afraid, so. I can't keep doing this. It's time I quit."

"I see," she said, and rising she excused herself to go to the ladies.

"Hell, Tommy. What have you just done? Are you sure?" asked Mac.

Doyle nodded his head. He had suddenly become aware of Veronica's reaction, although he was unsure what to do about it. "Yea, Mac. It's time."

It was sometime before Veronica returned to the table. When she did, neither Doyle nor Mac could tell that she had been crying. Putting a brave smile on her face, she pretended to yawn, saying, "Sorry guys. I think I'll call it a night. A girl needs her beauty sleep you know? Thanks for the dinner, Mac. I'll see you at the precinct before you leave. Goodnight, Tommy, good job done with Edward. See you around," and before Doyle could say good night she was gone.

Mac looked at Doyle, but didn't speak. Eventually Doyle said, "What?"

Shaking his head, Mac stood up ready to leave. "Missed chances, Tommy. Missed chances. G'night, catch up with you later."

As Doyle sauntered back to the brownstone, he pondered Veronica's reaction to his announcement. If he was honest with himself, he knew he had upset her. Was it the reaction he had wanted. Hell yes, but what good was it now. After all, she had been offered a good job at the hospital and he didn't want to spoil it for her. Better that, than her hanging around with an old has-been like him.

HEADLESS CORPSE

Doyle had been clearing his filing cabinet out. He'd already looked at many of the closed cases, passing them onto the lady who was typing them, ready for inclusion in a new training manual he was compiling. The aim of the manual was to assist new, up and coming PI's, and young Police Officers wanting to join the detective department in learning the craft.

He had spent the last few months having a good clear out, choosing the best cases and making sure there was a good cross section. He was considering retiring soon. After all, he wasn't getting any younger, thinking it was probably time he returned to his home town of Twin Peaks. It was to be the beginning of a new part of his life. There were things he still wanted to achieve away from the world of crime and now was the time to start doing them.

He would have liked a certain lady to join him; one Dr. Veronica Martin, M.E. However, since the dinner at O' Malley's following JoJo Grimondi's arrest, he had seen very little of her, as she was concluding her role as medical examiner at the local precinct. She was also due to start working at the hospital mortuary soon, so their paths hadn't crossed. Besides, Doyle hadn't worked on many cases since the kidnapping of Edward Carlton.

Mac was also working his time out up to his retirement on the twenty-fifth of this month. He was busy ensuring all his work was up-to-date. The new commissioner hadn't liked it when both Mac and the Doc had handed their notices in. Neither was the

Governor, who had practically begged both of them to stay. When asked why they were leaving, Mac's excuse was his retirement, and the Doc just said it was time to move on. Nothing more was said but they both believed the Governor was regretting his choice of Commissioner. Especially as the list of officers and other personnel, requesting transfers or taking retirement, began to grow. There was nothing he could do. He had appointed the man, so the buck stopped with him.

Sitting at his desk Doyle took out the latest batch of closed cases. He quickly scanned the ones he wanted to use in the new book, marking them for typing, then put the remaining ones in a box. Those not included in the book would be added to a catalogue to be donated to the Police Training Academy.

He had put the brownstone on the market and knew there was a lot of interest. This meant it wouldn't take long to sell it. Once it went he would no longer have any excuse for staying. Doyle sighed. Time to start the packing. He wouldn't be taking much with him, other than his personal stuff and a few bits of office furniture. The desk and chair could go in one of the spare rooms. He sighed again, wondering if he was making the right decision.

Suddenly the phone rang out. It's shrill sound pierced the peaceful Sunday morning. Doyle was tempted to ignore it but for some reason his second sense told him to pick the receiver up, as the demanding ringing appeared not to want to stop.

He almost snarled down the phone, as he sharply said, "Doyle."

There was a short pause, before a familiar voice said, "Good-morning, Tommy, sorry to trouble you on a Sunday but I could do with some help."

Tommy, recognising the gruff voice of Sheriff Thomas Jacks, replied, "That's okay, Tom. Don't often hear from you. What can I do? Is the house okay?"

Jacks was the local Sheriff at Twin Peaks where Tommy owned a house, so he was a little concerned that the place was okay. He hadn't visited the house for well over a month. With fires in the mountains being not uncommon, and the weather having been overly warm recently, you never knew what might happen.

"No, no, Tommy, the house is fine. Nick checked it yesterday while doing his rounds. It's another matter I wanted to talk to you about. I was wondering if perhaps you might be heading up this way in the next day or two?"

The Sheriff sounded a little disturbed so Tommy asked, "I wasn't, but if you need some help, Tom, you only have to ask. You know that. What's it all about?"

"Err... I wanted to run something past you. It's probably nothing, but seeing as how you've got experience, I thought a second pair of eyes on a case might help me. Do you think you could take a drive up? I can't promise you much of a fee, but we'll certainly feed you."

It was obvious to Tommy that the Sheriff was reluctant to talk over the phone, so he agreed to drive up that afternoon. As it happened he didn't have anything on at the moment so could spare the time away.

After he had hung up, Tommy went upstairs to pack an overnight bag. He then put a call in to his pal, Mac, Inspector Pete Mackintosh, letting him know where he was going. Then, turning the answer machine on, he set the alarm and drove away from the brownstone, waving to Pat O'Malley, who was cleaning the pub windows, as he drove by.

A few hours later, Tommy pulled up outside the San Bernadino Sheriff's station a mile off North Road, in Twin Peaks. Leaving the car, he breathed in the fresh air of the mountains, allowing the feeling of coming home to encase him.

It was bittersweet returning to his home town, and the house where he and Mary, his ex-wife had lived. 'You'd think after all these years I would be used to it by now,' he thought. The problem was, he knew it would take many more years before he would finally lay that particular ghost to bed. Or until she was replaced within his mind, and his heart.

"Tommy! How ya doing? Thanks for coming up. It's great to see you." As Doyle looked up he saw a grinning Sheriff Jacks standing in the doorway of the police station.

Locking the car, Doyle went forward, shaking the man's hands. "Good to see you, Tom. You're looking well. So, what can I do for you?"

Laughing, the Sheriff replied, "Whoa, Tommy, let's go get something to eat, then I'll explain everything," and turning he locked the office door, before turning back and leading the way across the road and down the street to a local hostelry.

The Antlers Inn was one of the longest standing historical buildings still open and operational in Twin Peaks. The outside looked as if it could do with some much needed TLC but the inside was another thing. Whilst the new owners had done their level best to retain the ambience of the historical building, they had also made it comfortable and welcoming for any visitor, or local resident to relax in.

As the pair entered through the old fashioned door, a short, rotund woman aged about 50 greeted them warmly. "Morning Sheriff. And... well, well, well - if it isn't Tommy Doyle. How are you, Tommy? It's been quite a while since we last saw you in here."

Doyle smiled. "Lucy Waters... you don't get any older, do you?"

"Or thinner," she replied laughing. "Lunch is it?" The pair nodded, laughing with her.

"Ahh," said Tommy, a glint showing in his eye as he told her, "but that means there's more of you to cuddle up to on a cold winter's night." Once again all three laughed, and despite her best intentions, Lucy blushed at Tommy's comment. If truth be known she had a soft spot for the tall handsome ex-cop, still not understanding why his wife Mary had left him. She certainly wouldn't have.

Settling down, they placed their lunch order. Finally, having waited patiently, Tommy said, "Come on, Tom, what gives? Why the hesitation? Tell me what the problem is?"

Although he paused before speaking softly, the Sheriff finally opened up. "We've found a corpse... a headless one. Out at the Community Church Cemetery."

"What's strange about that? Has one of the coffins burst? It's not unusual is it. Especially in this heat."

"No, that's true. The thing is, Tommy. It was found in a freshly dug grave. No burst coffin. The body just sort of appeared... over-night. It's a bit of a mystery and to be honest, I need someone with a bit more technical know-how than me and the boys have, to help investigate it further. So, I thought... maybe... you could help?"

Doyle didn't speak. 'Hell,' he thought. 'The Sheriff had as much call on technology and tech know-how as he had, so why would he need outside help? There had to be more to this than met the eye.' Deciding it might be better to leave the matter until after lunch, Doyle said, "Let's eat and then you can tell me, everything."

* * * * *

After a long leisurely lunch, Doyle and Tom spent the afternoon in the Sheriff's station going over the case, discussing what the Sheriff and the Deputies had uncovered so far.

As Doyle finished reading all the reports he sat back and let out a loud whistle. "Well, Tom, I see what you mean about not being sure what exactly you've got, other than a headless corpse. And, of course, the possibility of a mystery that is going to take some explaining?"

"Tell me about it, Tommy? Now you know why I asked you to come up. Do you think you can help."

Tommy thought for a few moments, then finally said, "Yea, why not. I've not got much on at the moment so I can spare a few days. I'll err... stay at the house and check in with you daily. How's that, Tom?"

Smiling, and breathing a sigh of relief, the Sheriff nodded his head, before saying, "Thanks Tommy. You're a life saver. Come on, I'll buy you some beers and food for the fridge."

Having paid the bill the two men left the inn and headed towards the local supermarket.

* * * * *

Later that evening Doyle was on the phone to Mac, explaining what the Sheriff had wanted and telling him he was staying at the house for a few days to try and help Tom sort out the case. Mac had been surprised, but as he knew Doyle liked the Sheriff, they went way back way before he and Doyle had even met, he wasn't that surprised.

What Mac didn't know, was that Tom was Doyle's ex-brother-in-law, and despite divorcing his sister, Tom had never let it affect his admiration of

Doyle as a cop. In Tom's mind, Doyle had always been a damn good cop. Unfortunately, his sister Mary had been a casualty of the 'force.' It surprised him even to this day how his own wife had stuck with him for so long. But, maybe that was because he worked in a small town area rather than in the city like Doyle had done. Less risk, less pressure.

Having agreed to keep Mac updated on what he found out, Doyle spent the rest of the evening going back over the reports. Climbing into bed that night he lay awake for a long time thinking about Mary and what had gone wrong between them. He knew it had been his fault. He had put the job before his marriage.

Sighing, his thoughts slipped towards a certain doctor; Medical Examiner, Dr. Veronica Martin. It was on that note he fell into a deep sleep, his dreams filled with visions of a slender body wearing a white hospital coat, with a red slinky dress beneath.

The alarm broke Doyle from a world he would have preferred not to leave. Opening his eyes he cleared his mind, realising he had to put the sexy M.E. away in a box, as now was not the time to become distracted. Rising he took a shower, got dressed and went into the kitchen to pour himself a mug of coffee. As he took the first couple of mouthfuls he started to come alive, ready to face the day. A plan was coming to mind. The first stop was to the local library, to do some research.

Parking in the car park of the Twin Peak Library, Doyle waved to Lucy Waters as she entered the Antlers Inn. Going inside the library, Doyle's first stop was the internet section. He wanted to check for any similar incidents of headless corpses. Had this been downtown LA then he would have headed for the precinct, asking Mac to check the records. After all, it wasn't uncommon for the local Mafia to drop their dead bodies in the cemetery. But not in a nice place like Twin Peaks.

Two hours, and lots of fruitless searching later, Doyle was no nearer understanding who could have dropped the body in the open grave. The strange thing was Tom still hadn't been able to tie down the fingerprints. Whoever the person was, or had been, they obviously weren't local. Which meant they were from out of town.

With this in mind, Doyle spent the next hour linking into the missing persons database. Mac had given him a special access pass to the listings to help him in his work. Unfortunately, this produced no results either. Doyle was beginning to feel frustrated, thirsty and hungry. He needed a break, so decided to pop across the road to the Antlers for a bite to eat.

Entering the inn he was surprised to find it fairly busy. As he walked up to the bar a few of the regulars who knew him, called out. They were all friendly, some teasing him, others offering to buy a drink or asking him to sit with them. Doing the rounds of saying hello, Doyle ordered a drink and a sandwich from Lucy. He took a seat next to a couple of old timers he knew who had lived at Twin Peaks for going on sixty years.

"Afternoon, Bob, Reg," said Doyle as he took a seat at the end of the bar close to them.

"Howdy, Tommy, you doing okay?" replied Reg. Bob just nodded his head. He never had been much of a talker.

"I'm not too bad, thanks," replied Doyle. "Rum thing this body in the cemetery, ain't it?"

Bob looked at Reg, and nodded his head again. Whilst Reg just said, "Sure is. You investigating it?"

Doyle nodded slightly, raising his glass in acknowledgement as if saying, 'sure am.'

"Mmm... rum thing it is," said Bob quietly.

"Don't suppose you have any thoughts on the matter, do you guys?"

Bob looked at Reg again, before Reg said, "Mmm... maybe. Depends."

Doyle didn't push it. Instead he raised his glass, pointing it at the Bob and Reg. "Same again, lads?"

Reg smiled a toothless grin. "That's real gentlemanly of you, Tommy. I'll have a beer. And Bob here'll, have a bourbon."

"A double," said Bob.

Doyle grinned slightly, before ordering the required drinks for the three of them. At the same time Lucy brought him his sandwich and one each for the two old men. "Why don't we go into the corner and chat?" suggested Doyle.

Bob looked at Reg again, nodded, then each, picking up their drinks and plates of food, went across to the table in the farthest quietist corner of the room. Doyle would not get any information easily.

And it would probably cost him at least two or three more drinks before he would finally leave the inn. However, when he did leave, he at least had more information to research into.

On the verge of leaving the car park, the sudden sound of a police siren stopped Doyle in his tracks. It also caused quite a few people to stop and turn to see who the cops had pulled up. They didn't get a lot of excitement in Twin Peaks, so, if the police were using their sirens then it must mean an arrest.

Getting out of his car, Tommy, walked over to the Deputy's motor vehicle. "You trying to scare the shit out of me, Nick?" he asked laughingly.

Deputy Nick Jacks, grinned. "Sorry, Uncle Doyle. But didn't think you'd seen me. Ma says you gotta come for dinner tonight, or else," and the young office laughed. He knew never to argue with his mother, but if there was man, other than his dad, who might, then it would be Tommy Doyle.

Laughing again, Tommy must have been thinking the same as the young officer. "Well, I'd better do as I'm told then, hadn't I. After all, doesn't pay to disobey her who should be obeyed, does it," and he laughed again as returned to his car. "What time, Nick?"

"Seven o'clock, Uncle Doyle."

"Oh and Nick! Stop calling me Uncle Doyle... its Tommy, right?"

"Right, Sir... Uncle Doy... Tommy," and Nick flicked the siren once more as he left the car park.

Shaking his head and chuckling to himself, Tommy returned to his house to wash and change. He also needed to drink a few good mugs of black coffee. Wouldn't do to get pulled over for being over the limit. Even Tom might have a problem with that. Maybe he should get a cab?"

Two hours later, Doyle arrived at the Jacks residence situated on the outskirts of town. There were three police cars parked out front, so there was no mistaking who lived here. In the end he had decided to take a cab.

Walking up to the door he pressed the doorbell, waited, then slowly pressed the door handle. Calling out, "It's Doyle," before going inside.

Suddenly he was accosted by two big balls of fur, followed by two youngsters, each yelling, "Uncle Tommy, Uncle Tommy," as they literally threw themselves at him. Before he knew what was happening, Doyle was on the floor being licked by the two dogs, and being bounced on by the two young children.

"Help, help," he called out. "I'm being attacked by some monsters. Someone, come and rescue me quick, otherwise I am going to have to tickle somebody a lot!"

"No, no!!" the twins screamed. "You can't. We win, we got you first."

"Okay, okay, you guys. Enough. Leave poor Uncle Tommy alone. He's an old man now and can't take you two, and the dogs bouncing on him." The voice was that of the twins Mother, Tina.

"Ahh.. Mom… Uncle Tommy doesn't mind."

"You heard me. In the room, now," their mother said, trying her best not to laugh at the sight of her Uncle lying on the floor.

With the kids gone, Doyle stood up and brushed himself down, before taking Tina in his arms to give her a hug and a kiss on the cheek. "By the way, young lady, less of the old man, please, or else I'll be tickling you," and they both laughed as they walked into the kitchen arm in arm.

"What on earth was all that commotion?" asked Sarah Jacks, Toms wife and Doyle's sister-in-law.

"The kids and dogs attacked Uncle Tommy at the same time. He didn't stand a chance."

"Oh dear, are you okay, Tommy," asked Sarah, sounding concerned whilst trying not to laugh.

Reassuring her he was fine, apart from a slightly bruised ego over something to do with being termed an old man, he gently kissed her on the cheek. Sarah was an older version of her daughter, Tina, and just as beautiful as the day she and Tom had married,

At that moment, Tom, Nick, and Chris, the Jacks son and son-in-law, came into the kitchen. Both boys greeted Tommy with gusto. They liked their Uncle, looking up to him as a fine example of what being a good cop should be.

The evening went well, with Doyle staying longer than he intended, but he did not regret it. The Jacks were the closest to family he had these days. He always enjoyed spending time with them, including the younger ones. He was also glad he had decided on taking a cab, having imbibed a little too much rum after the meal. He would sleep dreamless tonight.

* * * * *

The previous relaxing evening must have done Doyle some good, for the following day he arose with a clear mind and a solid plan of action. Tom rang with some good news just as Doyle was finishing his third cup of coffee. They had managed to locate who the dead body belonged to. The news surprised Doyle, but it also gave him a more positive outline for his research,

Once more he hit the library, this time visiting the missing person database but expanding his search wider. Within the hour he had hit the mark. The dead man was one Charles Vincent Armstrong the Fourth. He rang Tom with the details and told him he was continuing the search to find out if he could come up with anything else. Tom was grateful for any news, promising to meet up at the Antlers for lunch at one pm.

The rest of the morning, Doyle spent searching the dead man's name and history. By the time lunch came around he had gathered quite a pile of papers of printed matter from his internet search. Even Doyle was staggered at the collection.

Entering the inn, Doyle saw Tom sat at the bar talking to Bob and Reg. As he approached them, Doyle decided he would have a little bit of fun. Sitting down on the other side of the pair, Doyle said, "Hi guys, you two okay?"

Bob looked at Reg, who replied, "Yea, Mr Doyle. We're just fine. Can we get you a drink?"

"Why thank you, I'll have a double scotch over ice. You okay, Tom?"

"I'm just dandy, Tommy. And you?"

"Yea, Tom. You know that little job you had me do for you?"

"You mean the one to do with the headless corpse, Tommy?"

"Yea, that one, Tom. Did you know that these two guys here, were really helpful. They gave me such a lot of information."

"Well, I never," said Tom, feigning surprise. "Mmm... I wonder why they didn't give me any? What do you think, Tommy?"

As he said this Bob and Reg had started to rise but Tom and Doyle were ready for them. "Whoa boys. You're not leaving are you?" asked Tom.

Bob looked at Reg. "Well, we've got stuff to do, Sheriff."

"Mmm... like hell you do. You two are under arrest. You've got a lot of explaining to do. And I'm going to make sure you do start doing it now. Nick, Chris, you there?"

"Yes, Sheriff," the two deputies responded together as they entered from the kitchen.

"Take these two down the station. I'll question them after lunch. Okay, Tommy, what d'ya want to eat?"

An hour later Tommy and the Sheriff were sat in the Police Station discussing what Tommy had discovered so far. "I need to finish it off, or one of your boys can do it if you like, Tom?"

Tom looked at Tommy, before slowly saying, "To tell you the truth, Tommy, you've discovered a hell of a lot more than we ever could. Is it asking too much for you to follow through and finish it for me? I'll tell the Chief you did the work. Can't promise he'll pay you anything but I can at least try."

Tommy laughed. "Hey, I don't need paying, Tom. We're family. I help family, okay? After all a couple of Sarah's dinners will be payment enough. And your lads keeping an eye on the house for me. Pro rata, Tom, pro rata. Okay?"

"Thanks, Tommy. Well, I'd better get the two old lads questioned. Want to sit in?"

"No thanks. I'll get back to house and carry on. I want to check in with Mac. I've a couple of things I want to check with him. Fingers crossed, should be some good news," and Tommy stood ready to leave. At the door he stopped, saying, "Let me know if the terrible two spill anything of interest, won't you?" and he left as the Sheriff agreed he would.

Back at the house Doyle rang Mac, catching him just before he left for the weekly poker night with the lads from the precinct. He'd rung him earlier in the day asking for some information but so far no results. However, Mac promised to let him have what he came up with asap. Sending his apologies for missing the evening with the lads, Doyle rang off and settled down for the evening.

He had been deciding what to have for dinner when the doorbell rang. Not expecting anyone, he went to answer the door, checking through the side glass before opening the door. To his surprise he saw Dr. Veronica Martin M.E. standing on the doorstep. Opening the door, neither spoke for a moment, both feeling a little embarrassed.

"Veronica!"

"Tommy! I've managed to find the right house. Are you going to invite me in, or what?"

"Err... Yea... Come on in. Sorry. I have to say you were the last person I expected to find on my doorstep. How did you find me?"

"Mac told me where you lived. He said you were up here investigating a headless corpse for your Sheriff friend. And... as I was at a loose end I wondered if I could offer any help... Err... if you would prefer me to leave then I'll head on back..."

Looking at the one lady whose company Doyle knew he wanted to enjoy, he waited a moment, then stepping back, he smiled and invited her into the lounge. "I was just going to throw something in the microwave, want to join me?"

Veronica smiled. Removing her coat, Doyle took it from her, smelling her perfume, which reminded him of the last time they had spent an evening together. Following him into the kitchen, she said, "I don't suppose you have anything in your fridge, do you?"

Laughing, Doyle said, "Yea. My sister-in-law packed it full of stuff for me. I'll probably end up throwing most of it away."

"Sister-in-law?" queried Veronica, a little surprised.

"Married to my ex-wife's brother. He's the friend Mac was on about. They look after the house, and me, when I'm up here."

Despite herself, Veronica felt relieved. She had taken a big risk coming up here, not being sure how Doyle would receive her? Especially as they had not parted on the best of terms the last time they met. Since that meeting they hadn't seen each other, but she knew if she didn't make a move he certainly wouldn't and they would go nowhere. She wanted him, and she was sure he wanted her, but for some reason he was holding back. Almost as though he was frightened of her. She hoped not.

Turning towards the fridge, she opened the door and surveyed the contents. Finally, she said, "Right, well, I think I know what I'm going to make us to eat. How about you set the table, get some nice wine and I'll see you shortly. Erm... I presume it's okay for me to stay overnight, rather than my driving back? If not, then I'll just have water?"

Tommy, who was on his way to the dining room, paused for a moment. Then taking a breath, he said, "There's plenty of room. I've got err... four bedrooms. Not really sure why I hang on to it. So, yea, of course you can stay. I'll... go lay the table and check one of the bedrooms," and he smiled to himself as he left the kitchen.

Finding a pinafore in a drawer, Veronica lifted assorted items from the fridge and started cooking. Three quarters of an hour later she called out, asking Tommy to help her lift the dishes of food into the dining room. As they sat down, she was delighted to see how Tommy had put some candles on the table, some pretty place mats, cutlery, and a pair of delicate wine glasses. He'd opened a bottle of red wine to breathe. She was impressed at his style.

Dinner lasted a good hour, during which time Veronica and Tommy talked about lots of different subjects, yet avoiding discussing their forthcoming retirement plans. Tommy opened up about his wife, Mary. Veronica had known he'd been married, but this was the first time he had ever spoken about her. At least he wasn't bitter, accepting the job had been the main culprit in the divorce, him second. It wasn't as if he had cheated on her with another woman.

Having listened to Tommy being so open about his wife, Veronica felt it only fair to tell him why her engagement had broken off. It turned out that again the job had been the culprit. The long unsociable hours she worked, the friendliness of the guys she worked with, being called out at different hours of the night. Finally, they talked about them both retiring from their respective occupations.

"I didn't think you would ever consider stopping doing what you do," said Veronica.

Doyle looked at her. She really was a beautiful woman, and he felt a surge of desire start to rise in him. "I suppose with Mac going, it won't be the same at the precinct. And the last case with Edward really brought home to me that I'm not getting any younger."

Veronica laughed out loud, "My God, Tommy, you're not that old you know."

Smiling he said, "I'm in my early fifties. Time for me to stop whilst I'm on top. Anyway, luckily I don't need to work. Family left me well off. The brownstone has gone up in price. This house is paid for. I could sell this and buy something smaller, easier to look after. I don't cost much to look after. So hey, what the heck. Anyway, what about the new job, are you taking it?"

She didn't speak straight away, Wondering how far she could go. Finally, she said, "No, I aren't. I'm finishing at the mortuary at the end of next week. My leaving do is next week-end, if you fancy coming. I'm going to think about what to do next. I suppose I could do some part-time teaching. It's something I'm qualified to do. And, I've always wanted to write a book. I'm thinking about selling my place. Like you it's too big for one. It would mean I could afford something smaller, perhaps in a district like this. I have enough saved so I have no worries there," and her voice trailed away.

"Sounds a good idea. Some more wine?" she nodded yes.

By the time they had gone through the list of reasons why both their relationships had failed they had drunk the bottle of wine and a couple of bourbons over ice. Both were feeling pretty merry and very relaxed.

Standing, Veronica started for the kitchen. "I really should get the washing up done."

As she passed Doyle's chair, he grabbed her hand, saying, "Forget it, We'll do it in the morning."

Grabbing her hand had caused Veronica to lose her balance, and before either of them knew it she had fallen into Doyle's lap. Maybe it was the wine, or the smell of her perfume, or perhaps the closeness of her slender body that caused what happened next. For a few seconds time stood still, then slowly the pair moved towards each other and their lips met. The kiss was all they both expected it to be. As for the washing up; well, that was clearly forgotten.

* * * * *

The following morning as Veronica opened her eyes, she saw Doyle looking at her. For a moment, neither spoke. "Good morning, Dr. Martin."

Veronica smiled. "Good morning, Mr. Doyle."

Slowly Doyle, leaned in towards her. As their lips met, the desire for each other swelled once more and soon they were lost in a world of their own. An hour later, Veronica gently said, "I suppose we should get up. That washing up won't get done by its self. Will it?"

191

Doyle laughed, "I have an idea. Let's buy paper plates from now on. I can think of far better things to do than wash up," and he kissed her again, warmly and deeply.

* * * * *

As Doyle washed and dressed he smiled to himself. He hadn't felt this happy and contented since… since… he couldn't remember. Why had he waited so long, he asked himself. Last night shouldn't have happened… and yet… it had. And it seemed he wasn't the only one who had wanted it.

"Come on, slow coach, unless you're going to spend all day in there admiring yourself."

Looking up, Doyle smiled. Mac had been right, Veronica was one hell of a woman, and one who had the hots for him. And, despite his denials, he had the hots for her.

'Maybe I'm not as old as I think I am,' he thought as he turned back to the mirror, before saying, "Coming doc. Just wanted to make sure I'm awake, that's all." They both laughed.

With breakfast over, and the dirty pots washed, Doyle and Veronica set off to the centre of Twin Peaks. "It looks a nice place," she told him as they drove along.

"It is. Nice and quiet, with little crime. Which is why finding an headless corpse in a grave was a bit off-putting for Tom; Sheriff Jacks," replied Doyle.

Fifteen minutes later Doyle pulled his car up outside the Sheriff's Station. Leaving the car they went inside the building looking for Tom – Chris was on duty.

"Morning, Uncle Tommy," said the young deputy.

"Morning, Chris. Tom around?"

"He's just popped across the road, back in a mo. Hello," he said, rising from his chair having finally spotted Veronica who was dressed in a smart trouser suit, looking more like a model than the M.E. she was. "Can I help you, Miss?"

"Veronica, Dr Martin, is with me, Chris. She's the precincts M.E."

Chris blushed slightly having been caught out eyeing up the Doc. "Sorry, I thought you were looking for some help."

"I am," replied Veronica in her sexist voice, causing Chris to blush even more. "Do you have a copy of the local M.E.'s report on the headless corpse that I could take a look at, please?"

Doyle turned his face away, doing his best not to laugh out loud, as the young deputy, seemingly a little flustered, went across to the filing cabinet to get the required documents.

"Morning, Tommy," said a voice from behind them.

Turning, the pair found Sheriff Jacks, having entered through the door quietly, was eyeing the situation. After a short pause, he held out his hand. "You must be Dr. Martin, pleased to meet you. I would say Tommy has told me all about you… but, he's not. Shame on him," and he laughed out loud.

Veronica joined in. "A man of few words, is our Mr. Doyle, Sheriff. Pleasure to meet you. I hope you don't mind my coming and helping with the case?"

"Not at all. The more the merrier. And even better when the help turns out to be an attractive woman."

"Hey you, watch it, or I'll be having words with your Sarah about you," said Doyle, trying to sound a little indignant, whilst also trying not to laugh. "Talk about hustling in…"

"Boys, boys, no fighting please. You'll make this poor young man here… Chris, that's right, yes?" and the young deputy nodded, enthralled by what he was hearing. "Poor Chris will blush even more than he already has." And to take the sting from her comment, Veronica blew a kiss across the room to the young man who promptly did just what she had said he would… blush.

This resulted in all of them bursting into laughter, even Chris.

Once 'law and order' had been restored, Doyle, Veronica and the Sheriff sat down to discuss the headless corpse case. The doc studied the local M.E.'s and the other forensic reports. Finally, she told them, "Everything appears okay… except… did the M.E. discover what this small object was embedded in the top of the gut? There doesn't appear to be any mention of it in his report."

The Sheriff, then Doyle, each checked the photographs and the M.E.'s report. Veronica was correct. There appeared to be a small round object lodged in the gut, but no mention of it at all. Mmm... that was peculiar.

With no answer to give, Tom picked up the phone and rang the morgue. After speaking to the M.E. he was surprised by his response. "Are you sure," he asked? The answer obviously wasn't what he had expected but he couldn't argue over the phone.

Finally, he said, "Look Jim, humour me. Go through everything and see if somehow it's got overlooked. Or, maybe put in the wrong place. NO!" (he suddenly shouted) "I am not saying you lost the item, I am asking you... nicely... to check if you or one of your guys could have misplaced the item, that's all."

There was silence and from the look on the Sheriff's face he was not happy. "Double check... please. Look, I gotta go. People are in the office. Let me know. Bye." Without thinking he slammed the receiver down and swore loudly. "Hell, that man is an idiot. According to him, he never saw it. Can you get this man? No wonder he wears glasses... Humph... didn't bloody see it."

By now both Doyle and Veronica were literally rolling in their seats with laughter. They had come across many such incidents throughout their working lives, but Tom's reaction had been perfect.

Suddenly, the Sheriff looked up, stunned at their reactions. But, so infectious was their laughter that he swore again. "Hell fire, Tommy Doyle, this is not a laughing matter."

Doyle was nearly in tears, curled up with the fun of seeing his brother-in-law's face. Managing to control himself, he said, "Err… you are right, Tom. It isn't a laughing matter," and before he could stop himself he burst out laughing again. Despite himself, so did the Sheriff.

"Hell, Tommy, why did you retire, you could have been working up here with me and the lads. What a fun time we could have been having," and he continued laughing, slapping Tommy on the back as he did.

After they had eventually calmed down, the Sheriff decided he needed some lunch, so the three of them left the station, crossing the road to the Antlers Inn. Settling at a table, they ordered their food and drinks, before the conversation turned to more personal matters.

"So, tell me, Dr. Martin," asked the Sheriff, "have you been to Twin Peaks before?"

"Please, call me Veronica? And no I haven't. I was telling Tommy what a lovely place it appears to be. No wonder he has a house here."

Doyle didn't say anything, he just sat back, watching the interaction between the pair of them.

"Yea, it sure is. And Tommy's house is in a lovely spot. Isolated just enough, yet still within the community. We're a real welcoming community here."

Veronica turned, looked at Doyle, smiled, then turned back to the Sheriff. "It certainly appears that way, after the warm welcome I received." Doyle allowed a small smile to cross his face. If only Tom knew what sort of welcome he had given the doc!!

Lunch was a comfortable affair. At the end of it, Veronica excused herself to use the bathroom. As soon as she was out of sight, Tom pounced. "Wow, Tommy. Where the hell did she come from? You lucky old sod."

Doyle couldn't help but laugh at his brother-in-law's comments. "It's taken us some time to get it together. Seriously, what do you think. Mary was your sister."

Tom was surprised. Was Doyle still carrying a torch for his sis. He hoped not, especially as he still hadn't forgiven her for leaving Tommy the way she had. "Hell, Tommy. I don't care about Mary. She left you. She married you knowing full well what she was getting into, but she couldn't hack it. Come on, our own father was on the force. She saw what our mother went through. If she didn't want that for herself then she shouldn't have led you into marrying her... bitch."

Doyle was shocked. This was the first time Tom had ever shown any disapproval against his sister. He didn't know what to say. All these years he had felt guilty for allowing Mary to leave; not just him, but her family as well.

"Look, Tommy. This Veronica seems like a real nice girl, err... woman. I reckon she has a soft spot for you. As far as I'm concerned you take all she has to offer you. Get a life and enjoy it. You've spent too many years living on your own. Go for it."

"Okay, boys… and what are you being so conspiratorial about?"

Both Doyle and Tom looked up, as if caught out doing something naughty. "Err… I was just asking Tommy what you might think about joining me and the family for dinner this evening, over at our place. I mean, that is if you're staying up here for a bit. You're more than welcome. Sarah, my wife, would welcome some extra female company."

Veronica looked at Doyle questioningly. After a moment he nodded his head slightly, so she said, "I would love to, Sheriff, thank you. Err… do I have to bring him with me?" and she laughed as she pointed at Tommy.

Laughing, Tom said, "You'd better, or the wife will kill me. And please, call me Tom. Shall we say 7pm?"

Agreeing the time, Tom paid the bill, over ruling Doyle on the basis that it was the only way for him to get a fee out of the town. Then saying bye, he left, returning to the Station.

"So, Tommy, what are we going to do?"

Doyle thought for a few minutes. "As much as I could come up with a very pleasurable way to spend the afternoon, unfortunately I need to go to the library and do some more research. Pity, as I have a great jacuzzi that hasn't been used for quite a while," and he laughed.

"Boy, Doyle, you do know how to treat a girl, don't you?" and laughing they headed for the Twin Peaks library.

* * * * *

At dead on seven pm, Doyle and Veronica pulled up outside the Jacks home. Before getting out of the car, he turned to her and said, "Veronica, just so you know, Tom is my ex-wife's brother. Nick, also a deputy, is his son and Chris, whom you met, is his son-in-law. Thought you should know. If you don't want to stay we can go?"

Veronica looked at Tommy, thinking what a handsome man he was, and so considerate. Leaning across, she planted a kiss on his lips. "I'm sure they are perfectly lovely people, and won't eat me for dinner. Come on, Tommy Doyle, let's go in." She smiled warmly as he released the breath he had been holding.

As they walked towards the house door, Veronica shook her head, thinking, Tommy Doyle was such a strong man when it came to handling crime and criminals, yet here he was, acting like a date meeting a girl's parents for the first time. She was glad she had made the decision to take a few days off and join him up here.

As they reached the house, the front door flew open and Doyle was suddenly hit by two very excited youngsters yelling, "Uncle Tommy, Uncle Tommy, you've come back."

"Oh no... I've been captured by the terrible twosome. Help me, Veronica, they'll eat me alive unless you save me"

At the mention of Veronica's name the twins stopped grabbing Doyle, and stood stock still, staring up at the stranger. Slowly they moved behind Doyle's legs, hanging on to his trousers tightly.

"Wow," said Doyle. "If I'd known you could have that effect on these two I would have brought you up here ages ago." He laughed as he looked at the two children cowering behind him.

"Well, hello there, are you coming in or having a conflab on the doorstep."

Sarah Jacks stood looking at Veronica with curiosity. She was surprised, as in all the years since Mary had left, her brother-in-law had never shown any interest in another woman, never mind bring one to the house. Sarah liked what she saw.

"Kids… in the house… now. Sorry about that, come in? I'm Sarah by the way," and she smiled warmly.

"This is Veronica. A friend and colleague from the precinct."

Veronica returned Sarah's smile; from that moment on the two women became the best of friends.

Entering the house Veronica was quickly embroiled in the family, being warmly welcomed and accepted by the everyone. Slowly the twins got over their shyness, especially after they learnt what sort of doctor she was, and that she dealt with dead bodies. It appeared the kids were at that age were ghouls and monsters were the in-thing for them. Before long they were asking her questions about what it was like having to deal with dead people. This went on for a while until Tina had to finally tell them it was not a nice topic for the dinner table. Doyle watched the interaction between Veronica and the children, thinking how great she was with the kids. He began to wonder what sort of mother she would make.

'Hell!' thought Doyle, 'what the hell is up with me.' And he shook his head to clear his mind of such ideas.

By the time Doyle and Veronica left, the rest of the evening had gone with no hitches and lots of laughter. Saying goodnight the pair returned to Tommy's house. However, after they had driven away there was quite a conversation in the Jack's house about Tommy suddenly producing a beautiful woman whom he was obviously attracted to. Despite that conversation they were all happy for him, wishing him the best for the future.

* * * * *

The following day, after another enjoyable night, Doyle and Veronica left Twin Peaks. They travelled up country to further investigate the origins of the deceased, Charles Vincent Armstrong the Fourth. The intention was to discover as much as they could about the man and his demise. Heading north towards Santa Clarita, Doyle drove for some time, happy in the companionable silence. Finally Veronica spoke.

"Can I ask you something, Tommy?"

Doyle was silent for a moment, concentrating on the road, finally he said, "Sure. What do you want to know?"

Veronica knew she was taking a risk, but despite her confidence, she needed to know if there was going to be a future with Doyle. If not then she would stop it now and not get further embroiled with him. Eventually, she asked, "Do we have a chance?"

"A chance?" Doyle sounded surprised, or maybe confused. Deciding it might be better to pull over he slowed down and edged into the side of the road. Having stopped, he turned to look at her, asking, "Are you asking me if you and I can have a possible relationship? Or, if what has happened the last couple of nights is just a one off?"

Veronica laughed lightly. "Hell, Tommy, you know how to get to the point don't you. Well, yes. I'll be honest. After what happened with Mickie, I am wary of getting involved with someone again. If this is just a one night stand then I need to know. Look, I like you Tommy Doyle. I like you a lot but I don't want to get hurt again, so I would like to know where I stand. That way I can either decide to stay, accept it's an on/off thing or just walk away." Her voice trailed off as she suddenly felt foolish.

For a moment Doyle didn't speak, staring ahead out of the windscreen as he tried to gather his thoughts together. This was the last thing he had expected her to say; having honestly thought she was about to reject him. Telling him that the last couple of nights had been a mistake. Slowly he let out the breathe he had been holding. Then turning he looked her straight in the eyes.

"Veronica, I cannot say where we will go from here. I haven't been interested in any woman since Mary left me. She hated my job; couldn't cope with the long hours, the risk etc. That still applies whilst I'm doing the PI stuff. I suppose the reason why I'm thinking of retiring. Plus, I've been living on my own for a few years now. I've err... probably got some bad habits, although overall, I'm fairly well house trained." He paused, Veronica, choosing not to respond, waited patiently for him to continue.

"Hell, Veronica, I like you too. I like you a hell of a lot. These last couple of nights have been fantastic. I'll be honest with you. Yes, I want it to continue. But, I can't tell you what the future will hold. I can't say to you, yea we can make it, or that we'll be great together. If I'm truthful, I would like to believe we could. But, who knows. Also, the idea does frighten me a little. So, all I can promise you is this: If you want to give it a try... well... I would like that. I'd like that very much indeed. To share my life with you. But, it's down to you, Babe."

Veronica relaxed, breathing out slowly, before turning to face him. As she looked at him she smiled, "I would like that very much too, if that's okay with you?"

Leaning forward, Doyle kissed her gently and smiled. "So, now we've sorted that out, can I carry on driving? We've still got some work to do. The rest we'll sort out later to night, okay?"

Laughing she nodded, replying, "My God, aren't you the romantic, Tommy Doyle? Come on then, let's go, Boss." And Tommy quickly kissed her again, before starting the car and carrying on to their destination, a big smile plastered across his face.

Just south of Santa Clarita, Doyle turned off the highway up a small dirt track leading towards an estate. Half a mile up the road they passed between two gate posts. A sign stated, 'The Captain Charles Armstrong' Estate & Museum, Private Property – Museum closed until further notice.

The buildings were about a mile further up the track. They pulled into the car park out front of the Museum. Doyle, parking the car, looked around. "Looks like we've arrived," he said. "Come on, let's go see what we can find."

Leaving the car, the pair walked towards the building sign-posted Museum. Doyle tried the door but it was locked. "We'd better go look at the other buildings. There must be someone around otherwise they would have had those gates locked and bolted."

"Shall we split up?" asked Veronica.

Doyle shook his head. "No, better not. Just in case. You never know. Sometimes people can be sensitive to strangers and get gun happy. Can't do with losing you having just got you, can I."

Veronica smiled, following his lead.

"What do you want? Can't you read – the museum is closed," snarled a gruff voice.

Doyle and Veronica slowly turning, discovered an old man in what appeared to be work clothes. He was standing and pointing an old shot gun at them. Not normally one to be shocked, Veronica turned white. Doyle held his hands up. "Sorry, Sir, I was looking for the owner. We are making enquiries on behalf of the Sheriff of Twin Peaks and wondered if the owner of the estate was available please?"

The old man looked first at Doyle, then Veronica. "You got some ID?"

"I have but I need to put my hands down to get it," said Doyle.

"Okay, go ahead, but no funny business."

Slowly Doyle reached inside his jacket and pulled out his PI Identity, before offering it to the old man to look at.

"I'm a Medical Examiner with the LA Police Force," said Veronica a little nervously. "Would you like to see my ID as well?"

The old man looked up at her. Deciding she was okay, he handed Doyle his ID back, saying, "No. That's okay. The owner isn't here. Haven't seen him for over a week. Very strange, very strange. I's worried about him."

"Would his name be Charles Vincent Armstrong the Fourth, by any chance?"

The old man looked at Doyle. "Yea, that's him. You know where he is?"

Doyle took a moment to answer, looking at Veronica before doing so. "I'm sorry to have to tell you, but Mr Armstrong is dead. His body was found in the Twin Peaks cemetery about six days ago. The Police have been trying to discover who he was which is why I am here. I act on behalf of the police sometimes. And, as my colleague says she is a

Medical Examiner so she has an interest in viewing the area here, if that's okay with you?"

The old man didn't answer. He was shocked at what Doyle had told him. Not quite believing that his master was dead. "What happened?"

"That's what we are here for," Veronica explained softly. "To try to find what could have happened. We know you've had a shock, but can we look around, please?"

As the old man looked up at her, there were tears in his eyes. "Of course, of course," and he led the way to the museum. "He was a good man, not like his son. Mr Vincent was always good to me, he was."

Doyle and Veronica looked around the museum. The exhibits related to Captain Charles Armstrong who had been a hero during the Mexican – American Conflict. In the final months of the war the Captain had been in charge of a group of locals who had defended a settlement from a command of retreating Mexicans being chased by the Americans. The Captain had been wounded while attempting to stop the Mexicans from burning the settlement to the ground, firing round after round alongside his small group of militia, and stopping the Mexicans from escaping until relief came.

The museum showed the history of that day's events, being full of mementos. It had been the idea of Mr Armstrong's late Grandfather, but the current Mr Armstrong, the deceased's son, had no interest in the museum. Doyle was to discover that the son had argued with the deceased a couple of weeks prior to the man's death. The reasons being that the son wanted to close the museum and pull all the buildings down. The land was worth more than the museum. To the son the contents were just old rubbish.

"Tommy, look here."

"What have you found?" asked Doyle as he crossed the room to look.

Joining her at the display case, he looked to the spot where Veronica was pointing. "Well, well, well. Now that's interesting. Well spotted my girl," and he kissed her lightly on the cheek, then opening the case he took a clean handkerchief and removed a couple of the exhibits.

"Err… you can't take them," said the old man.

"I'll give you a receipt for them. They are going to the Twin Peaks Police Station. They will be returned after they've been tested. I'll also leave you my card and contact details. If you want you can ring the police station and confirm with them that I have the right to do this?"

The old man hesitated, not sure what to do. It wasn't until Veronica said, "You do want us to find out what happened to Mr. Armstrong don't you? I promise we will look after them, and we will bring them back. I promise."

Seeing her smiling at him the old man finally agreed that it was okay.

Having viewed the museum, Doyle asked to look inside the homestead. To Veronica it was very much a man's home. There wasn't a female touch anywhere. Nothing. It was almost sad, and for a moment she could picture that if and she Doyle didn't work out then that could well be him in a few more years. She wouldn't let that happen to such a good man. Whether Doyle had similar thoughts no-one knew. Perhaps it was fortunate that Tommy couldn't read her mind.

As they were leaving to return to Twin Peaks, Doyle reminded the old man not to tell anyone, especially the son, of their visit. Or that he had removed anything from the displays. Although surprised by the request, the old man readily agreed.

It was late when they got back to the house. Doyle rang Sheriff Jacks to bring him up to speed while Veronica made them something to eat. While it was cooking she went to take a shower. With the phone call over, Doyle sat in the lounge thinking over the conversation he'd had with Veronica earlier in the day. It wasn't that he was afraid of trying to make a go of it with it Veronica. She was after all a very beautiful, desirable woman and certainly good in bed. The question that bothered him most, was whether or not he was good enough for her? Could he stay the course and satisfy her needs? Not financially but romantically?

"You look lost in deep thought there, Tommy. Having regrets?"

Looking up, Doyle's breathe was taken away at the sight of Veronica in her black two piece nightwear. He stared at her for a moment in silence, taking in how voluptuous she looked, feeling a stirring deep in his loins. Then he whistled loudly.

"Perhaps you should turn the oven off?" he said smiling at her. "If the aim is to get me to lose weight you're going about it the right way," and he laughed.

Laughing she crossed the room and sat next to him. "Are you having regrets? Second thoughts about us?"

Shaking his head, he took her in his arms. "Not about you, darling, but about me. Are you sure I'm what you want?"

Slowly she lifted her hand and gently stroked his face, before leaning in to kiss him gently on the lips. "Hell, Doyle, do you think I'd have dressed up like this if I'd had any doubts about you?" The rest of the evening was lost and the meal ruined.

* * * * *

The evidence Doyle had picked up at the Museum was handed over to Sheriff Jacks who sent them away for forensic examination. Over the next couple of days whilst they waited for the results Doyle and Veronica researched Armstrong Junior. Discovering more about the argument the father and son had had about closing the museum and selling the land. It appeared that the Armstrong estate was prime building land and worth quite a fortune. Mr Armstrong Senior wasn't interested in selling. He was wealthy enough in his opinion, so didn't need to sell his home or give up the family heritage for the sake of earning a few dollars.

The son, however, was greedy and lazy. His father had sent him off into the big bad world to earn a living but he had failed. This was put down to his mother having spoilt him as a youngster. The parents had divorced when he was ten years old, the wife receiving a good settlement which she had squandered. She wasn't poor for long, remarrying another man of wealth fairly quickly, so the boy had grown up getting everything he wanted. This information would be an important element in the investigation.

Whilst Doyle had been up country, Sheriff Jacks had been investigating further the small round object showing in the deceased's throat that had been missed by the local M.E. After some days of searching, the object suddenly turned up, having been found in a local pawn shop. The unusual nature of the object is what had drawn the owners attention to it. This in turn had led him to contacting the Sheriff. Two days later the young man who had pawned the item was arrested. The case was slowly coming together, much to the satisfaction of the Sheriff.

Five days after Veronica had arrived in Twin Peaks, she joined Doyle and the Jacks family for dinner at the Antlers Inn. "Her treat," she said. "As thanks for their warm welcome." Tomorrow morning she was returning to the city and to her last week at work. Doyle would follow her in a few days, once the case was finally closed. The evening went well with all the Jack's family cheerfully asking her to return to see them anytime – with or without Doyle. Veronica was deeply touched. Doyle and Veronica's last night together was also a delight, with them not getting to sleep until the wee small hours.

* * * * *

The following morning Veronica reluctantly returned to the city. The parting from Tommy had been hard. He had held her in his arms and kissed her long and slow. She hoped the time apart would allow him to confirm to himself that he wanted their relationship to go forward, as much as she did. She drove away with some trepidation and the odd tear in her eyes. If she had looked back she would have seen the smile on Doyle's face. A smile of satisfaction and one of happiness. There was his future, if she would have him. He knew when he returned to the city he would have to risk taking the chance. Yet, he felt it was a chance worth taking, for he believed she felt the same way about him as he did her.

After Veronica had left Doyle threw himself into helping the Sheriff complete his investigation. The son of the deceased, Philip Armstrong, was located and brought into the Twin Peaks Sheriff's station for questioning. He was every bit as arrogant as he had been described as being. Unfortunately for him, Tom Jacks may well have been a rural Sheriff, but he was every bit the tough cop Tommy Doyle had always been' especially when it came to dealing with over entitled culprits.

Finally, all the pieces of the investigation came together. Entering the interrogation room Sheriff Jacks and Doyle were met by Armstrong's lawyer demanding an explanation as to why his client was being held. He also wanted to know who the hell Doyle was.

Sitting, the Sheriff waited until the man had finished talking, and then in a firm voice instructed him to sit. "Interview with Mr. Charles Philip Armstrong. Present Mr. Coulter, legal representative for Mr. Armstrong, Sheriff Tom Jacks and Special Investigator, Mr. Tommy Doyle. For the record Mr Doyle is on loan from the LA Police Force and is acting under my orders as Sheriff of Twin Peaks. Now Mr. Armstrong I want you to explain to me all about the argument with your father, Mr Charles Vincent Armstrong the Fourth on 17th June last."

"That's none of your business," replied the young man.

"Are you refusing to answer the question, Mr. Armstrong? You do appreciate this will not look good!" said the Sheriff calmly. Doyle was ready to hit the young man for just looking cocky, never mind what came out of his mouth. 'Good job I'm off the force,' he thought to himself.

Despite the Sheriff's calmness the interview went from bad to worse. Armstrong was being arrogant, his lawyer was trying to settle him, and the Sheriff was losing patience. Finally, Tom said, "I think we'll take a short break. Interview halted at…"

"Does that mean I can leave," asked Armstrong standing, grinning.

The Sheriff stopped in the doorway. "No - it does not mean you can leave, Mr. Armstrong. It means you are under arrest on suspicion of murder and will be removed to the police cells. Oh! And by the way, there will be no bail. Our Governor doesn't like suspected murderers lose on the streets of Twin Peaks. An officer will come, read you your rights, and process you. You will be housed in the Twin Peaks Jail; you may even possibly be removed to LA County Jail. You have been non-cooperative, and as the LA County representative, Mr. Doyle has the say on whether or not we keep you here or move you." On that note Doyle and the Sheriff left.

Back in Tom's office, Doyle looked at his brother-in-law. "Thanks for the promotion. You do realise you won't get away with that?"

Tom laughed. "Well, sorry to say, Tommy lad, I already have. Besides, I spoke to your friend Mac not long before we went into the interview. He agreed that if I needed an ace, then you were it and he would back you. Apparently he got the Governors blessing. So, sorry pal, you're mine at the moment."

Doyle laughed. "You sneaky bastards. I'll have a few words with Mac when I get back. But, well played, Tom, well played! By the way what about the two old boys, Bob and Reg?"

"Doing them for illegally disposing of a body. They coughed up quite a bit of information. The only thing we haven't got is the head. God knows where that it is. We're hoping it will turn up but I'm not holding my breath. It may well be lost to the wild life."

"What about Armstrong?"

"Gonna let him stew overnight. If we don't break him tomorrow, he's yours to take back to LA and Inspector Mackintosh. Come on, let's go, Sarah is cooking us a nice meal, and I've been told to make sure I don't go home without you. By the way, expect to get the third degree about Veronica," and Tom laughed as he led the way out of the Station.

Arriving at the Jacks home, Doyle was greeted more warmly than usual. The twins threw themselves at him eagerly, and for once he didn't mind. At least while they were around he wouldn't be bombarded with questions about Veronica. However, the inevitable could not be put off for ever. Once dinner was over and the kids had retired to bed the questions began.

"So, Tommy, tell us all about Veronica? How long have you known her? How long as this been going on?" asked Sarah before anyone else could jump in.

"Ahh… come on Sarah, give the guy a break. Are you trying to embarrass him," said her husband?

"I want to know. He's never brought any woman here before. Besides, I like her."

"Sorry pal, I tried," said Tom looking at Doyle.

Yawning, Doyle tried saying, "Well, I'm bushed I think it's time I retired."

Only to be met with calls of, "Oh no you don't. Sit down, Tommy Doyle," from Sarah and Tina.

Surrendering to the inevitable, Doyle said, "Okay so I will tell you, but then I don't want to talk about it anymore in case I jinx it… okay?" Reluctantly the two ladies agreed, sitting back ready to listen, as did Doyle's brother-in-law who was also eager to learn more of the beautiful lady M.E.

Doyle explained how he knew Veronica, that they worked together, that when Mac had needed help, he and Veronica had gone undercover on an investigation. He told how they had a mild flirtation with each other. Finally, they both realised they were attracted and Veronica had taken the initiative by coming up these last few days and pushing the boundaries. They had talked it over and decided they would give it a go. He told them they had talked about him having been married to Mary, and Veronica being engaged to a guy called Mickie. They agreed that the job had affected both relationships so had been wary. But, as they were both going to retire, they were willing to give it a try to see where it went. And that was it. End of.

"Wow, is that it?" asked Chris, Tom's son-in-law.

"Yep, that's it," said Doyle.

"Well, I am happy that you found someone, Tommy. You make sure you make it work. You need someone to make you as happy as I am with my lovely husband here, even if he's never around to dry the dishes," said Sarah laughingly, as she snuggled up next to her husband Tom.

Doyle promised her he would, and that they would see more of them in the future as they would probably move into the house. The whole Jacks family were delighted.

* * * * *

The following morning Philip Armstrong was once more shown into the interrogation room. This time he was a little more subdued, probably due to an overnight stay in a not very luxurious police cell. The interview went well. Armstrong tried denying any involvement in his father's death, that was until Tom showed him the coin retrieved from the deceased man's throat. Armstrong didn't say anything, but he looked at his lawyer who had also remained a little more subdued. When asked if he knew what it was, Armstrong admitted it looked like something similar to those in the museum. At this point Tommy took over the interrogation.

"Actually Mr. Armstrong, it is one from the display cabinet. As is this one and this one. Two of these I removed from the case when I visited the museum a few days ago. The third one was found at a pawnbrokers, stolen by a young man."

"Well, there's your murderer then, yes?" said the lawyer.

"No. He stole it, after it had been taken by a young intern working in autopsy, once it had been removed from your father's throat during the post mortem. When we questioned him, he was very forthcoming as to why he took it," explained Doyle.

Going on, he said, "You forced this coin down your father's throat, causing him to choke. Having murdered him, you needed to get rid of the body. However, as the coin was lodged in his throat you tried to get at it by cutting of his head. Despite your

216

efforts you still couldn't get the coin out. You decided to dump the body and head in the forest, hoping a lion or black bear would come along and maul it, thus losing the coin."

"Unfortunately for you," Sheriff Jacks spoke, the body was found by two old boys, Bob and Reg, who were out poaching. Being religious men they took your father's body and dropped it in an open grave in the cemetery. Unfortunately the head had already disappeared. However, the coin has a fingerprint or two on it."

"You can't prove it was me. My fingerprints will be all over those coins. I helped set the displays up," snapped Armstrong.

The Sheriff looked at Doyle. "Do you want to tell him or should I?"

"It's your case, Sheriff. I think you should tell him."

Smiling at Doyle, Tom nodded his head and looked back at Armstrong. "Well, you see that is where you are wrong. It appears, that just prior to you arriving on the day you had that argument with your father, he had spent the previous few weeks cleaning and cataloguing the inventory of all the items in the museum. You see your father was going to put his collection on display at the State Museum, so he needed to check and value everything. After each piece had been catalogued, they had been cleaned and only handled wearing white gloves. There was no way any fingerprints, not yours, your fathers or anyone else's could possibly be showing on these

217

coins. Not even the ones borrowed by Mr Doyle here, as he used a clean cloth to remove them. Strangely, the only fingerprints found on the one coin was yours. Even the young man who stole the coin knew not to touch it, as did the pawn broker, which means you, Charles Philip Armstrong, are under arrest for the murder of your father, Charles Vincent Armstrong the Fourth."

With that Doyle and the Sheriff stood up and left the office. As they left two policemen from County State Jail entered, placing Armstrong in handcuffs, before removing him. He was last seen, and heard, shouting at his lawyer to do something to get him out this mess. Unfortunately for Armstrong, there was nothing the man could do to help his client.

Holding out his hand, Doyle said, "Well done, Tom. Great job."

Shaking the proffered hand, Tom smiled, "Couldn't have done it without, Tommy. If you decide you want to come back on the force I'd welcome you any day."

Shaking his head, Doyle said, "Thanks, but no thanks. It's been fun, but as said I'm rethinking my future. Hell, it's not as if I have to work. It's time to rethink my priorities. Probably going to come back and live in this place. What do you think?"

Laughing, Tom said, "Whatever you do, Tommy, you're always welcome. And, if your future involves that lovely lady of yours, then go for it, Tommy, go for it."

Doyle smiled, saying, "I will, Tom, I will!

EPILOGUE

It's been six months since the Headless Corpse case. The brownstone stands empty, bearing a 'sold' sign above the door. Tommy was pleased with the amount he received.

Following his return to town he decided to let Mac know that, at last he and Veronica had, in Mac's words, got it together. Mac was delighted, although he had already guessed the reality of the situation when he met Veronica on her return and saw how happy she looked. More so, when she mentioned how she'd met Tommy's family.

Veronica's leaving do had been a great night, with her receiving lots of gifts and well wishes for her future. When asked what she would be doing she had informed people she was moving north to write a book. The hospital were, of course, disappointed that they hadn't managed to snare the best medical examiner in the state. But she had agreed that once she was settled she would be willing to give the odd talk to prospective new doctors and forensic scientists, so they were happy. The Governor too found that he had some big shoes to fill when it came to finding her replacement. And was even more disappointed when she told him where he could put the pay increase he had offered her. Not a very ladylike response was Tommy's laughing comment.

Mac's celebration for his retirement had also been an evening of joy. At least for Mac. The only people who did not enjoy the night was the new

Commissioner, and again, the Governor. The former, although invited, had the good sense not to attend. And the latter was left feeling stupid when he realised what a good man he had lost.

The week before Doyle left the brownstone, the locals had gathered at O' Malley's Bar & Grill to say goodbye to Tommy. They had welcomed him to the area and he had proven to be a sound influence on the local youngsters. Often teaching them the right and wrong way of doing things. Law and order had ruled in the area so he would be sadly missed.

Doyle, Mac and Veronica had one final meal together at O' Malley's Bar & Grill. As they sat eating and drinking, they chatted about what the future held for each of them. Mac, having sold his apartment, had found a small house in Twin Peaks with a small workshop attached, not far from Doyle's house. He was going to start a small carpentry business. Doyle would be his first customer as there was some work to do on the house he owned.

"So, Veronica, how's the house sale going?" asked Mac.

"I've got a buyer for it. A nice young couple. It's going to make an ideal first home for them," she replied.

"That's great. So what you gonna do, next?" he asked.

Veronica looked at Doyle, who smiled and nodded his head slightly. But before she could speak, Tommy said, "Well, actually, Veronica is going to move in with me!"

Mac didn't speak. He was surprised and yet not so, as he had expected this to happen.

Veronica said, "We do have something to ask you, Mac."

"Err… yes, sure, what?"

"Tommy and I wondered, seeing as how you are his best pal, if you would like to be his best man?"

Mac, stared at her, then at Tommy, who was smiling at him, before turning back to Veronica, then back to Tommy. Finally, a big grin spread across Mac's face. "Try the hell from stopping me. Come here, you old devil," and standing up, he gave Doyle a big hug.

"Hey, less of the old!" said Doyle, laughing.

"Congratulations, you sly old dog," said Mac wrapping his arms around Doyle and whispering, "Good on ya, Tommy lad, good on ya."

ABOUT THE AUTHOR

Ann Brady is an award-winning author of historical fiction, as well as of Children's Picture Storybooks and other genres. Being a speaker and writer's mentor of many years standing she is now lovingly known as the Fairy Godmother of budding writers.

Doyle's Casebook was one of Ann's first forays into the world of fiction writing after spending many successful years as a non-fiction writer for an award-winning website, as well as international magazines, national newspapers, and educational tutorials. Writing is her joy and passion, and she likes nothing more than sharing her knowledge with new and developing writers of all ages.

Details about Ann, her writing and her books can be found on the following websites:

www.ann-brady.co.uk

www.annbradybooks.co.uk

www.littlefriendsbooks.co.uk

www.dearfriendsbook.co.uk

Ann's books can also be found on Amazon and at all good bookshops.

Details of Ann's work through Mentoring Writers can be found on their website. She works as a writers mentor assisting writers worldwide to understand, learn, and discover the joys of progressing their own writing journey towards being a successful published author.

She also works with the Kids4Kids Organisation a charity she set up some twenty years ago to help young people. This she did initially through the element of sport, but these days through writing. To date Kids4Kids.org.uk has mentored several children, publishing quite a few of their manuscripts.

If you need help with your writing then you can contact Ann through the following websites:

www.mentoringwriters.co.uk

www.kids4kids.org.uk

This book along with many others has been published under the imprints of Pen & Ink Designs or Kids4Kids.org.uk details of which can be found on the publishers website.

www.penandinkdesigns.co.uk

www.ingramcontent.com/pod-product-compliance
Lightning Source LLC
Chambersburg PA
CBHW071505170626
46811CB00007B/2740